I0721772

Northern Rose

ROSELEEN WALSH

WORKBOOK PRESS LLC
187 E Warm Springs Rd,
Suite B285, Las Vegas, NV 89119, USA

Website: https://workbookpress.com/
Hotline: 1-888-818-4856
Email: admin@workbookpress.com

Ordering Information:
Quantity sales. Special discounts are available on quantity purchases by corporations, associations, and others.
For details, contact the publisher at the address above.

ISBN-13:   978-1-954753-09-9 (Paperback Version)
                978-1-954753-10-5 (Digital Version)

REV. DATE: 10/02/2021

Chapter one: Bad News in Belfast

She ran, leaving the door open and tripping over the small child playing with books on the floor of the waiting room; her body taking over as her mind blanked, unable to cope with what the doctor had just told her.

Twenty minutes earlier her life seemed predictable and certain, so certain that before her two o'clock appointment, she had put in for a five hundred pound loan from the Credit Union. Her annual pilgrimage to Fundoran for a week long ration of passion, country music and Bacardi with a dash of coke was only a day away and Gloria was counting the hours. Mrs Jess from the Clonard Credit Union smiled as Gloria sat comfortably in the tiny partitioned cubical where her loan request was being processed. Looking over her oval shaped spectacles the frame of which matched her eyes, Mrs Jess joked with the hearty laugh that by now all the customers came to expect; (though first time borrowers didn't know how to respond because the joke wasn't always obvious to them!)

'I just knew it was about time you would be looking the money to go for your week in what you may call it.......

Bun.. Bun… oh yes……….. Bunbeg!'

'Wrong this year again Mrs Jess, its Fundoran I go to, not Bun Bun Bunbeg but Fundoran, Gloria laughed. You know where all us country fans flock, to do our own thing and to be ourselves for the week!'

Mrs Jess smiled and gazed into Gloria's brown eye. She preferred the brown to the blue and it was to the brown eye that Mrs Jess each year would stare in amazement. Gloria usually made only one personal appearance to the Credit Union each year; her daughter Glory B would come in faithfully on her mother's behalf each week after ward to pay off the loan; Gloria usually managed to have the loan paid off two weeks before she would put in for the new loan.

It was a feature that drew most attention to Gloria. People never really seemed to get used to the fact that she had two different coloured eyes and Gloria's eyes were usually the first thing that anyone noticed about her. She often said it was like an ice breaker, you know how it is when you don't know what to say to someone you meet for the first time, and well Gloria's eyes were certainly something to start a conversation about.

'Where are you off to, Gloria?' and without seeming to take another breath, 'Julie hasn't been in yet! Is she not going this year?' Mrs Jess, according to Julie, always spoke in a nosey parker voice. Gloria gave her a serious look before replying curtly, 'Hardly, she met a fella last time and he broke her heart…. twice! She's a real sucker for men with gum decease, know what I mean, the false teeth were a dead giveaway. The top set clashed with the bottom set every time he spoke and it doesn't bear thinking about when they made mouth to mouth contact……yuck! He was hardly discrete either wearing a cheap toupee; the laugh of it was that it was all so obvious; then lifting her eyebrow said 'know what I mean… the only Julie thing about him was that the toupee was blond; she goes for blond men in a big way! I mean when do you see a 40 something with natural blond hair these days…anyway, she's not going to Fundoran. She had a slight windfall (Gloria was careful not to elaborate on where the windfall came from as Julie was slightly embarrassed about the whole incident) no, she's only going to the birth place of them all.'

Mrs Jess dropped her pen and exclaimed out loud 'You don't mean, The Grand Old Opera in,' she couldn't quite remember the name so she gestured with both hands trying to prompt Gloria to finish the sentence.

'Yes' nodding her head, 'you've got it in one, the home of them all, the birth place of country music!'

'You don't mean Graceland's!'

'No Mrs Jess, you're thinking about Elvis, the king of them all, I'm talking Hank Williams and Nashville Tennessee, there's a subtle difference and it's all to do with legs and how you move them'. They both laughed and then continued with the loan application. Finally Mrs Jess went off to the other room to get approval for Gloria's £500 loan and Gloria's only concern at this moment was how much she was going to miss Ali her boxer for a whole week. Ali, a pup of 9 months and beautifully marked was Gloria's reason for taking daily walks. She made so many new friends these past months, everyone seemed to notice Ali and they'd stop her and ask how old the pup was and what its name was, and she'd never tire of telling Ali's story of how she got her name. People would be surprised to discover that Ali was female and not male like Muhammad Ali the world's greatest boxer according to Gloria. She just loved quoting him at every opportunity and this week her favourite quote was 'don't count the days - make the days count' and in another hour those words would be more than relevant.

Handing her the cheque Mrs Jess bid Gloria a wonderful time and said she'd see her the same time next year. Gloria walked her self-confident, happy walk, through the busy side streets of Clonard and crossing the busy Springfield road where she'd no time to respond to the wolf whistles from the lads who weren't aware just yet about political correctness or of the accusations of sexual harassment or the fact that whistling after an attractive girl in the street would soon become extinct in West Belfast. She practically danced down the Springfield and into the doctors. She couldn't have been happier or in better form.

As she sat in the waiting room Kathleen Gillen's 3 year old was pulling the empty chairs around the floor, much to the annoyance of old grumpy Mr Toner, he was tut-tutting aloud. Gloria remembered what it was like taking her boisterous Glory B to places where they had to wait. She tried to distract this bespectacled, notorious moaner, for Mr Toner the groaner was well known in the Hilltown estate. People said he just didn't like children, although it didn't occur to anyone that an old man of almost eighty might find it hard to put up with constant loud music at all hours from neighbours, plus the daily destruction of his cottage garden by children searching for their footballs. It never occurred to Gloria either but she would try to sooth the situation.

'Waiting long, Mr Toner?' she pretended to be concerned.

'Too long' came the reply from the agitated professional moaner!

'What time are you here from, Mr Toner?'

'I've been here over an hour and I'm feeling worse now than when I came in. I've a migraine. I'm not able to sit in waiting rooms any more. He should have come out to see me instead of all this sitting around getting your eardrums blasted by blooming children' he moaned.

'Excuse me, you old moaner' said an aggrieved young mother 'but my child has the right to play if she wants. She's not doing you any harm. She's not even near you' at that, the surgery door opened and the older Doctor Smyth popped his head round the door and summoned Gloria to come in. She happily obeyed, ignoring the tutting of both Mr Toner and Kathleen Gillen, for nothing could annoy her today of all days, or so she thought.

'Right Gloria, how are you feeling?' Enquired the doctor as he checked his desk for a sheet of paper which had URGENT marked across the top.

'Great doc, just great, on my way tomorrow to my annual retreat, my ration of passion and my Ooh la la and as Ali once said, 'Don't count the days – make the days count' – that's my motto for this week and I'll live every moment like it's my last…………' There was a strange silence as

Gloria waited for doctor Smyth to laugh, instead he looked at her holding this A4 page, he glanced down at the page and said, 'Gloria, this is the results from your scan………'

'Right, I see'…. She said eagerly 'the scan… why don't I like your tone doc?'

Silence and then Doctor Smyth looked briefly at the A4 page as he let it drop on the desk top.

'There is no gentle way to tell you, Gloria, but the test results aren't good' He looked her in the eye and held her hands her tiny hands in his, rubbing them to ease the shock of what he was about to tell her. 'It's your scan results, they show that you have a tumour……….'

'A what……….'

'A tumour, Gloria, I'm so sorry, so, so sorry…'

'A buckin tumour……….. How did that happen? How did I get that?' she yelled into the doctor's face. He responded by holding her hands tighter but Gloria couldn't be held, she tugged her hands free and yelled again 'a buckin tumour how in hell did I get it….'

'Gloria….the worst kind…you can try surgery but it's a…….50-50 chance'…..that was all she could make out, now everything, every word the doctor spoke every action as he stood up all seemed to be in slow motion. It's a dream it's a dream a voice in her head kept saying………. before she realised she was running along the Falls road holding the A4 page that out of nowhere had sentenced her to death. Some unknown person says that she's going to die and because her doctor believes it, so must she; not likely! If she could run forever then she can't die, death will never catch up with her, all these thoughts flooded her mind and then in the blink of an eye she couldn't see where she was going; she was like a pigeon with an inbuilt radar directing her flight path back home to where she knew she lived and would be safe from lies. She was hearing this other voice in her head telling her to breathe, breathe, breathe, keep breathing don't stop, you only went for the stupid scan to get a stupid claim, you weren't even hurt………. you only tipped your head on the dash board………. The car wasn't even going fast! The voice continued in her head but this time it was her own voice. I don't believe this……….. this is all made up…….. it's a joke……….. I can't die…………. not now……………….. I've too much to do……… there's too many things I need to do, to do…….I'll go to bed and then get up and start all over………. this is a dream ………..it has to be. One minute everything was in slow motion and the next it was like watching a video that was being fast forwarded or like sitting in a train that was going too fast for your eyes to focus on the scenery; green door…… green door………..

it's here somewhere.................where's my house........ her mind raced until she reached the only green door in her street!

Opening the front door she expected Ali to run and greet her; she so needed that ever faithful boxer to jump out and overwhelm her with soppy licks and paws all over her; she remembered then that she had left him earlier in Colligan Street with the Watsons   where she would be well looked after for the week. None of this was real, how could it be? There was no build up to it, she'd been feeling fine, no headaches no nothing unusual!

As she climbed the stairs for once failed to notice the torn wallpaper that had hid the blue marker drawing of herself done proudly by a three year old Glory B; fourteen years ago she had cried and scolded Glory B that cold December night as they headed for bed. The hall and stairway had only been decorated a week or so, Gloria wanted everything nice for Christmas; the paper was red with gold stripes and Gloria had to do double shifts in the chippie to pay for it and the doll's house that Glory B would treasure along with her Cindy doll. Gloria never got the hall redone, it was a conscious decision and the reasoning behind it was so she would never forget how harsh words can break a three year olds heart, even if the three year old doesn't understand what the words mean. Going upstairs many times since had forced Gloria to hold back her anger and the temptation to say unkind words to her beautiful daughter.

Before throwing herself into the king sized bed which was positioned carefully so she could experience (if she so wished) her piece of planet earth move slowly past the moon's light without fail each evening; she found it reassuring in her darker moments to belong in a world that was both consistent and never ending and then to be greeted each morning with the sun's rays (a cloudless sky permitting) coaxing her to enter into the day's magic; on a good day she would open up like the snowdrop or daffodil or one of her pink roses, ready to give and receive what the day had to offer. But now she closed the bright orange silk curtains that set the room aglow each day like a blazing sun somewhere in an African desert; today this room would become not her oasis but her tomb.

After sometime she reset her Joe Dolan CD to usher her into her dreams or as it happened this beautiful afternoon……….. her nightmare.

Chapter two: Good news in Boston

Henry Dickson was middle aged and the father of Kelly an eighteen year beauty pageant queen who was hoping to study law at Harvard; they sat side by side as though they hadn't a care in the world; Kelly picking at the white tips of her perfectly manicured and lacquered nails; they even looked at one another as they spoke; no one would guess that the opposite was the truth. How could anyone guess that Henry was waiting to see his doctor to hear what he thought was almost a certainty; conformation that he had a brain tumour. It could be nothing else he had told Kelly, four weeks earlier, preparing her for the inevitable; he knew only too well about headaches and tests. Both, his father John O Neill and his younger brother Patrick, had both died from brain tumours; Henry's mother remarried and changed his name to Dickson when his stepfather legally adopted him. It runs in the O' Neill side of the family, he told Kelly and for once she actually listened to what her father was saying; his words becoming muffled and distorted in Kelly's head there in the tiny room where she had been a prisoner those past weeks.

'Your grandfather's grandmother my great grandmother, Rosena O' Neill, apparently her brother had some sort of a tumour, I guess then and back in Ireland they didn't have many hospitals and ill people were nursed at home until they died, what I mean is nothing was ever looked into to see if it could be corrected or something.' Kelly didn't cry, she was too shocked, how could she cope with this news, how could she cope without him. By the way, I forgot to mention that Kelly was in rehab at the time, she had a serious drug problem, so really this bad news was the catalyst for her recovery. She had been in denial since she was fourteen, it was ironic, Henry thought, that his death might pull his daughters life back together and start to mean something to her; for the past few years she seemed to have a death wish that she was determined to make come true!

'What am I supposed to do dad, curse the O'Neill's for having this weakness? Maybe they had other weaknesses as well............ maybe addiction! Any of the O'Neill's die from addictions?' This was a serious question not just a quip. 'When I get out of here I'm going to find out who I am and who I come from!'

'You know who you come from, Teresa Malone and Henry Dickson, the luckiest guy in the world to have married her and created you! Right?'

'Right - but you know what I mean, my minds been all over the place in here, I really need to know exactly who

I am, I want to know and now if anything happens to you……..'

'Yeah, well then we can find out together.'

Kelly held her father's hands in desperation and rubbing her thumbs up and down his palms then lowering her face, her sad expressionless young face, to be cupped and caressed and held like a priceless jewel. It had been so long since Kelly had felt emotion of any kind; she would look in the mirror and see only a strangers face that had the look of death about it, no smile no expression just the blank stare that said, don't touch because I can't feel, don't push because I can't move, don't love 'cause I can't love back. But at that moment, feelings in her stirred; the sudden gush startled her like a blood transfusion starting at her toes and rising to her head; like the sleeping beauty being wakened, not by a kiss but by pain. The pain of feeling something, was both wonderful and yet terrifying; a tear trickled on to Henry's palms and he felt like a miracle had happened; lifting her face, which until that moment, had the hardened features of an addict, but now, his daughter who was dead had come to life again. He too had died many times and without hope of resurrection; my God, he thought, my death will be worth it if it gives my child back her life. They were both locked in a moment of grace, a moment when hope triumphantly cast every doubt they had ever known eternally to that dark and lonely place of despair where every soul who suffers addition knows only too well.

The last time Henry and Kelly had embraced was when Kelly's step mum walked out without a word leaving them both to find out from neighbours that she'd been having an affair with the local gardener, Deano Rodgers; they ran off together to make a new life for themselves in New York, for Cathy, Henry's second wife, was encouraged by her lover to become a movie star. They had no money and even less talent; Cathy definitely had the looks, if that was all it would take.

Kelly's mother had died in an automobile accident when Kelly was six years old. The whole neighbourhood went into both shock and mourning. Henry met and married Cathy within the year. Cathy needed somewhere to live, and everyone, except Henry, knew that she had played Henry along. She was a very good looking woman and a lot younger than Henry; she modelled herself on Marilyn Monroe; the only routine in her life was the twice weekly visits to Stefan's Hair and Beauty Salon, where she would be given the works by Stefan himself and claiming that theirs was a business arrangement whereby she was his model and he paid her in kind! But perhaps Henry used her as well, for he needed someone to look after Kelly while he worked all the hours he could trying to build his printing business from scratch; Henry seemed oblivious to what was going on under his nose and eventually under his roof!

In a moment of desperation Henry grabbed hold of Kelly's hand and said in a whisper 'Tell you what princess, regardless of the outcome in here as soon as we get home I'm making plans for us both.'

'What sort of plans, you're not going to get me committed again …. are you'? They both smiled, and he kissed his daughters cheek as the love he felt for her burned within. She was her mother's daughter and this special love, he thought only father's feel for their daughters, burned at this moment in this bazaar setting like an eternal flame; it had certainly only flickered in recent times but now it burned brighter and stronger than ever before and it was a beautiful sight to behold this bond between a father and daughter. The other patients quietly waiting and eaves-dropping all glanced at the father and daughter while silently hoping that he would hear good news from the god in the next room!

The buzzer went on the intercom and the receptionist half smiling told Henry that the doctor was ready. Henry took a deep breath as his six foot frame stood up and confidently moved to the door. Kelly went to follow her father but he motioned for her to stay in her seat.

'Wait, wait there, this won't take long!' and their eyes locked for that final split second. The door closed and Kelly's life was put on hold.

Chapter three:
Die now or wait till later

The July sun lit the room and blazed through the orange silk curtains that weren't made to hold the day at bay. Gloria's life thus far was transparent, what she appeared to be she was and no one could ever put her flighty spirit down, some had tried and ended up with a sore jaw or red face! Her five foot two inches deceived those who would take advantage. Gloria wasn't an aggressive girl but in new situations she always had to stick up for herself; she was never mealy mouthed. As she sat up and turned Joe Dolan back on she realised her daughter had turned the c.d. player off when she came home in the early hours, after finishing her shift in the Belmont Hotel, a job she didn't particularly like but it was better than the dole for now. Glory B was planning to go back to college in September to get her A levels in French and Business Studies. She was hoping to go to university and then to travel abroad working in different hotels, it would be a good way to see the world and get the experience she needed. She was an ambitious girl who was expelled from school wrongfully accused of smoking dope in the school yard the previous year, she was allowed to complete her G.C.S.s and got 5

As and 4 Bs. Gloria acknowledged that the school had permitted her daughter to complete the exams because they knew she was innocent; but she refused to name the guilty party so they wouldn't let her back. 'Life's a bitch' Gloria told her daughter at the time, she didn't encourage her to tell the name of the girl, but advised her always to do what she knew to be right. Would history repeat itself on Gloria's daughter! Gloria knew what it was like to be accused in the wrong. She was with foster parents at the time, Sally and Jimmy, they were good people but the welfare thought she'd be better off in the stricter routine of the orphanage.

Strange, she thought sitting there on the edge of the bed, it's like déjà vu, I've faced death before, the last time it came out of the blue just like this, I survived, stretching to put on her silk red dressing gown she remembered, remembered only afterwards, and the trouble, getting accused in the wrong and having to go back to live in the orphanage. It had been a lovely summer's day, just like yesterday she uttered out to herself, she could see quite vividly the rocks and the blue sea that deceived both school girls, one from a family home and the other from a borrowed home; the sea lapped in and out of the side of the cave where they had gone for a sort of picnic with boys from school. It turned out not so much a picnic, though they had mars bars, kit-kats and stale sandwiches; but more a first drink initiation, and the drink was cider, the big brown plastic litre bottles.

They were both 14 and the boys were of a similar age; that Wednesday was their entrance exam to the gang; if they passed by getting drunk and being able to get home without parent trouble then they would be accepted into the gang. But events over took their membership when Jeanie after a few gulps of cider felt dizzy and in an attempt to throw up over the edge of the rocks, she leaned a bit too far and fell, crashing into the sea, everyone clambered over and just stared in disbelief. Gloria screamed for someone to go in after her, but no one moved, then instinctively Gloria ran and jumped into the water to save her friend. Jeanie was unconscious and heroically Gloria was able to pull her to safety. Her reward from Jeanie's family was alienation, they blamed her on leading Jeanie astray, after all Gloria was only an orphan, the welfare were informed and again Gloria was punished by being sent back to the home, broken hearted because although her best friend was alive, she'd lost her and any trust she had in adult judgement. Now at this moment when everything seemed so normal she sighed and said out loud, 'who'll save me, who'll jump in and take me somewhere safe!'

She quietly made her way downstairs; in the kitchen she went to fill the kettle but changed her mind and filled the percolator instead, for she wanted the rich aroma of Kenyan coffee beans to fill the house like it did when she was small. The smell never failed to bring her back to the best of times in her emotional memory book. She'd been a very happy child: homemade soup on Sunday's with the Sunday roast, fresh cut grass on sunny days and the sound of brass bands practicing in the parochial hall were all constant things in Gloria's childhood, nothing changed until she was eleven when her parents died in a car accident and Gloria and her two brothers were placed in an children's home. Then everything changed forever. All the joy and happiness had gone. It was seldom she scrolled back through the years, but now she sat and wished with all her heart that her mother would suddenly appear and hold her and pat her face until everything was all right again, everything back to normal. She played that trick on herself in the orphanage when she felt that lonely surge come over her; pretending her mother was there was the only thing that ever eased her pain; but she also knew how lucky she'd been after all she had two brothers and they all shared their parents who loved them for eleven, thirteen and fifteen years, other kids in the home didn't have all that love behind them; most of them were there since birth.

Gloria's memory was like a bank with a savings account and also a current account; a bank that saved her emotions; recent and distant; a smell or a mood would unlock them, though not often nowadays.

Gloria didn't hear Gloria B coming down stairs; she was in another world staring at the percolating coffee oblivious to her daughters' presence until she nudged her and asked what the occasion was for the coffee percolator in the middle of July. Gloria grabbed hold of her daughter's hand and squeezed it, 'what's up with Gloria today? I'll rephrase that' she joked, 'what's up doc, this here hour of the morning when all good folks should be fast asleep in the land of nod, the sun hasn't seen you this early in years!'

Mother and daughter looked directly into the other's eyes,

'Ma Jones otherwise known as the local gossip observed you at precisely 1.30 pm yesterday and you looked like the storm troopers were after you, what happened, did you do a robbery or something, the credit union perhaps, she also observed you going into the doctors at 1.55pm precisely, now what have you to say in your defence, mam' she nudged her mother trying to gently coax what had happened out of her, 'I looked in on you on my way up stairs this morning, but you were fast asleep and Joe was singing his heart out. What's wrong, is there something you need to tell me, tell me anything Gloria except if your pregnant' she joked again trying to dismiss the feeling that she was about to be told something really shocking. What could it be, they didn't keep secrets, she knew her mum wasn't seeing anyone so it couldn't be that she'd found out she'd been having an affair with a married man, what was it. 'Mum, Gloria, whatever it is I need to know. Then like the speed of lightning Gloria said, 'I'm going to die, I have a tumour and it's as simple as that the doc says so, and that's that'! Putting her head on her daughter's shoulder she closed her eyes and sighed.

After a moment Glory B asked in a quiet voice 'Why are you so calm, is this a joke? I'm the joker here not you. You're not for real Gloria. Look at me' her voice quivered as she lifted her mother's face from her shoulder and searching her eyes looking for a hint as to why she would play such a rotten trick on her, but there was only an avoidance in her mother's eyes. Glory B broke away from her mother's hand and ran out to the back yard to scream to heaven and to wake up.

It had been the strangest morning ever and it wasn't even 11 o clock yet, well five minutes to go; they both sat facing one another on their 4th cup each of Kenyan percolated coffee and not a memory surfaced between them, it was a time for forming what they would both look back on as a new emotional memory.

'How can they be sure?'

'I don't know how can they make a mistake like this, I saw the letter, it's real, o.k.' Gloria answered in a humdrum tone that her daughter was not accustomed to hearing from Gloria.

'What happens now? What are we going to do?'

Gloria looked into her daughters eyes and said, 'We're off to Fundoran, you and me, and we're going to have the time of our lives that's what we're going to do!'

'Don't be daft, you have to go back to the docs and see what the next step is, what tablets you'll need, or whatever, we can't just up and go, everything has to be put on hold till we know exactly what's going to happen to you.' Pausing for a moment and still looking into her mother's eyes she said 'Gloria, this isn't just like the time you broke your arm, remember!'

'Yeah, I broke my arm breaking into here, that was a right mess you got me into, I wasn't to know that the ladder was wonky, served me right for taking it without asking, but you'd think our window cleaner would take more care of his equipment, but I've always been lucky with bad luck, I mean things could have been worse, I could have broken my back that time so breaking my arm wasn't all that bad! Gloria sighed and her daughter didn't like it when she sighed, there always seemed a hopelessness about when Gloria took deep sighs, and this time there was good reason for her sighing.

'I don't like it when you sigh'

'It's just a little thing I do unconsciously, just a family trait, I think'.

At that Gloria Stood up and in her typical matter of fact way told her daughter to pack a few things that they were catching the two o clock bus to Fundoran! Glory B was reluctant to argue with her mother, so she did as she was told, in a hurry, and packed make-up; underwear, summer tops and jeans into a smallish pink suitcase on wheels; anything else she could buy when they arrived. Gloria struggled down stairs with her extra-large pink suitcase on wheels; she had everything she needed neatly packed two days previous, the only things she had to add were the hair dryer and straighteners. She looked around the house as though she was leaving it for good. She closed the curtains perhaps to keep the light of days ahead out from her life until she would be ready to return and resume her life in whatever form that would be.

Gloria turned the key in the door then pushed it twice as always to make sure it was locked properly, the phone started ringing and Glory B wanted to go back to answer it in case it was her work, but Gloria refused to unlock the door and said optimistically 'if it's important they'll ring back'; they looked at one another, began to pull their cases behind them and walked the short distance to the bus station as though they hadn't a care in the world. As the bus left the station Gloria fixed her ear phones, turned on her Walkman and listened to Joe Dolan for the entire journey; Glory B listened to the quietness of her heart and knew that before long both hearts, hers and her mothers, would be in turmoil when this short journey was over.

Chapter 4: The Irish Connection

Looking down on the clouds from so far above induced a feeling of insecurity in Kelly, she felt frightened and uneasy; an irony that was not wasted on Henry, for he could remember an occasion the previous year when Kelly believed she could fly after taking crack at a beach party; she climbed to the top of some rocks, they really weren't all that high but she thought she could fly and flew off like a bird leaving the nest for its first solo flight and crashing into the water below. A life guard pulled her to safety and resuscitated her; she was hospitalised for two weeks that time and was lucky not to have been committed indefinitely. Even a broken arm didn't deter her from taking drugs, the reality of what might have been didn't seem to frighten Kelly; but it terrified Henry.

Kelly closed her eyes and griped Henry's arm tightly, 'what's wrong sweetheart?' he said softly

'I'm freaking out dad, I'm afraid to look down, I've got that falling sensation, you know like I'm just going to fall any minute!'

'That's only to be expected on your first flight, think logically, the changes of something happening up here are overwhelmingly minute compared to travelling by road!'

'I know, I know that dad, but sometimes fear is more to do with instinct than with common sense, what do you say?' Just then the plane shuttered and the lights flickered as the pilot made his announcement that they were going through some turbulence and that all passengers should remain in their seats and fasten their seat belts until further notice! Gripped with fear, both arms were now tightly holding onto the far arm of Henry's seat and her head dug into Henry's groin. She was whimpering like a little lost puppy but Henry felt no concern for this turbulence in the sky, but instead appreciated Kelly's need of him; it had been a life time since she last reached out for the comfort of her father's strong arms and he embraced the moment willingly.

'Are we going crash, dad?' he heard her whisper as he stroked her forehead in an attempt to sooth her trembling body.

'Now, now princess, don't be foolish', he mimicked for her to shush with his lips and continued stroking her forehead.

'So sorry for everything' she mimicked back. He understood and felt happy; he also knew that it was only turbulence and they would be through it before long.

Kelly was so like her mother Teresa, she too was terrified of flying and that was the reason why Henry had never been to Ireland before; going and finding out about his roots had always been something that he had longed to do. Now he was on his way and his mind raced ahead wondering what he might find: would he find anyone from the O'Neill side of the family still alive in Donegal; the hidden explorer in him would no longer be contained within his easy-going manner, it was out, as his daughter would soon discover to her amazement!

Henry lifted Kelly to an upright position back over in her own seat, 'just take deep breaths, that's right, now again and again, shush, shush everyone's frightened, we'll be through it soon, it's just pockets of wind, that's all, just little wind pockets, trust me, I'm your dad, nothing's going to happen'.

She closed her eyes so tightly it felt they were going to pop out until finally as she calmed down the plane hit another pocket of wind, this time the moved slightly to the left and everyone screamed and sighed, the plane felt as though it was in free fall, but in fact the pilot was dropping height to get out of the path of turbulence.

Henry really wasn't concerned, he'd had his wake-up call only days before and the bonus was that he had his daughter back. He'd lost his wife whom he'd loved all his life and still did; Cathy didn't matter, losing her at the end was a kind of relief, but losing his daughter to drugs, that was something else, even if the plane were to crash, he had his daughter back and he would die happy for that reason. That wouldn't make sense to anyone who always had their child to love and keep safe, but when a parent loses a child, not to illness or death, but to addiction, self-destruction and to the street, then that is a loss that may not seem like a loss to anyone but the parent. The nightmare of losing Kelly to addiction was over for now at least; but with any addiction, Henry knew recovery has to be one day at a time and there could be no certainty concerning anything beyond that!

Henry looked at his daughter as the pilot announced that the turbulence was over and passengers could open their seat belts; cheers rang out as the TV screens came on with some country singer in concert singing to the jubilations of all the passengers. 'There now princess, told you it would be fine, just rest, we've still a long way to go'; out of nowhere in Henry's head came a voice reciting part of Robert Frost's poem, Stopping by Woods on a Snowy Evening, he looked at Kelly as she closed her eyes, at last calm and content, and this inward voice recited over and over;

'The woods are lovely, dark, and deep,

But I have promises to keep,

And miles to go before I sleep,

And miles to go before I sleep'.

Henry held his daughter's hand, closed his eyes and rested; no sleep touched him for the rest of the journey in case she would need him again.

.

Chapter 5: Fundoran

It was late afternoon when the bus pulled up; the sun blazed down on the tarmac yard leaving a sticky residue of tar on soles waiting for the luggage compartment to be opened. Gloria and Glory B were last to disembark, the freshness of the sea air stimulated Gloria's memory, she thought how any other time on arrival she would run to the wall that separated the bus depot from the sand and would take in deep breaths of that fresh salted air and think how wonderful it always was to be in Fundoran for this special week; the excitement of the festival would have her on a high the moment of arrival. Now she stood like a woman far removed from this beautiful day, like someone in a trance and who possibly wouldn't know how to enjoy herself if the opportunity were to come her way; this was the complete opposite from what Gloria was really like!.

'Gloria, brighten up, we both agreed to ……you know what….. until next week' her daughter said in a soft caring tone as she put her arm around Gloria to gently move her forward to where their suitcases had been left by the bus driver on the soft tarmac.

'I need help to get my head round this' she said without

looking at her daughter but gripping her hand so tightly whispered 'don't let me let go……… promise'.

There was so much Glory B want to say, but it would have to wait, she could hardly think straight herself, her priority at this moment on this magnificent day was to get her mum to the hotel and settled and then ……whatever!

Mrs Kelly, the land lady of 'The Country House Hotel' a smallish building off the main street and not listed in the tourist guide for the area of recommended places to stay. In fact it was debatable as to which category Mrs Kelly's establishment fitted into, was it a small hotel or a large boarding house? Whatever it was there could be no disputing that Mrs Kelly was the local queen of country, a title she earned as a young girl who not only looked remarkably like Patsy Cline but also sang like her as well. Today she sat as she usually did during this week behind the reception desk wearing her cowgirl suit and matching hat, she looked like the real thing and so gave the guests the impression that they had arrived at the right place…… The Country House Hotel was the country fan's place to be! She greeted both Gloria's with a genuine smile and a kiss on the cheek, 'your room's ready Gloria, great to see you kid' she said to Glory B eyeing her up and down and wondering if the young girl would be competition to her status as country queen remembering that Glory B did a good impression of Dolly Pardon. 'Where's Julie'? She enquired softly in case Julie should suddenly appear with both arms weighed down carrying the different country outfits on hangers she had brought along to every single festival week for the last 10 festivals. Mrs Kelly was the sort of lady who knew everything about everybody; she was well suited in her occupation. Guests, especially when intoxicated, tended to trust this kindly faced lady with their deepest and darkest secrets; though it has to be said, she repeated nothing, and over the years her guests always came back, she was a lady of integrity, an agony aunt of sorts, even the men trusted her, and one such man was indeed the 'toupeed' blonde who lassoed Julie last year.

'Julie's away to Nashville this year…. are we in our usual room?'

Mrs Kelly noticed Gloria wasn't her usual bubbly self, she glanced at Glory B and handing her the room key said,

'Number 33, hope it's cool enough Gloria, I didn't open the windows this morning, I know how you suffer from hay fever and the pollen's very high at the moment'.

'Thanks' Gloria said feebly, 'we'll talk later' and off they both went up to the top floor pulling their matching luggage up the three flights of stairs.

'I love this room, the view's magnificent, look at that sea, it never changes, always there, always the same………now it feels like it's a video and someone's about to turn it off'

'Please Gloria, mum, don't talk like this, you promised, I promised, I'm not going to let you down and you have to do the same for me, one week can't make all that much of a difference now, can it? We'll forget the last 24 hours….. at least till we get home'. Glory B realised how much this week at the festival would mean to both of them if things got bad. They needed this week to hold on to, things may not be as bad as they seemed right now, after all miracles happen and there was no reason why one couldn't happen to them.

'O.K.' raising her hand 'I promise, the last 24 hours, which amounts to my bad news, will be locked away in my pink suitcase as soon as I unpack it, it shall be left locked outside on the veranda where it shall remain until the day of our return… back to reality; now that's that, a promise made and a promise to keep!' They threw their arms around one another and held back the flow of tears that was bursting to cry out. Gloria locked the veranda doors and pulled the flowered curtains closed tightly so no ray of light could seep through.

The weather was a hectic 28 degrees, it was impossible to keep cool. The two Gloria's went scouting on the beach for the usual good looking guys that the festival attracted, everyone did the same, it was all a bit of fun. Most country fans enjoyed living the dream for that week. Gloria was dressed in a blue gingham shirt tucked down a skimpy pair of denim shorts, she carried her sling backs in hand and ignoring the beads of perspiration trickling down her neck refused to take the cowboy hat of her head. Glory B looked stunning in her white blouse knotted above her pierced belly button, her brown hair in plaits that fell just above her full breasts that were generously revealed by the unbuttoned white blouse. The red and white stripped shorts looked fantastic hanging from her hips and for the first time ever Glory B wasn't embarrassed by her sexiness, she knew she had it and now in the security of being in her mum's company she intended to flaunt it. The two girls lapped up the wolf whistles as they strolled along the declining tide of purest white foam that came and went like the beat of a heart, effortlessly. Glory B, every so often, stopped to untangle the seaweed from her ankles conscious that she was probably the object of fantasy for all the young males disguised as harmless and innocent boys grouped along the beach protecting their lower halves from the blistering sun with beach towels.

'Hi Gloria, where's Julie?' a sixty something in a cowgirl bikini shouted from the side of a tent pitched on the camp site to their right,

'Hi Jean, you're looking good girl, Julie's gone to Nashville to live the dream there, haven't heard from her at all must be enjoying herself!' Gloria stopped as Jean slid down the sandy bank; they both opened their arms widely, embraced and kissed one another's cheek.

'How do you stay looking so god dam good missus zippy'? Gloria asked in a serious tone.

'When you've got a lover like mine, you have to stay looking good, otherwise you might lose him to someone looking better' she joked back but Gloria knew it was the truth. Sam, Jean's husband, had an eye for the girls, he wasn't restricted by age either, he liked women of all ages, though maybe that was obvious as he was at least 30 years Jean's junior. Jean was a beautiful looking woman, she had a good hairdresser who could make her blond hair still look natural, and the blue colour of her eyes were enhanced by the blue eye contacts she wore. The first time Gloria and Jean had met around 5 years ago, Jean had advised Gloria to get either brown or blue eye contacts so her two eyes would be the one colour. Promising to meet up after the variety show, where country greats like Joe Dolan would be the main attraction; they embraced and went their different ways, Jean back to her tent where her young lover waited and the two Gloria's back along the beach once again eyeing up all the talent that lay around like puppies in a pound, barking mad in hope that they'll be picked by two loving arms and pampered!

Suddenly as they neared the main street black smoke came tunnelling its way beyond the rooftops distorting the cloudless sky as it shot. There were two loud bangs like explosions and then flames. Some people ran down towards the smoke, others stepped into shop doorways too frightened to move any further. Glory B's instinct was to run towards the billowing smoke, she grabbed her mum by the hand and led her to a clear vantage point where they could see what actually was on fire.

'It's The Clarence' people started shouting as they ran up the street

The fire brigade made up of local volunteers, the resident doctor and two nurses who had been on their way to the Letterkenny general hospital all rushed to the scene. The two Gloria's stood well back from the crowd as the Garda sealed off the entrance to the hotel grounds. The fire was clearly at the back of the hotel, 'it looks like the restaurant, maybe that was a gas explosion we heard' Gloria said, turning to where her daughter had been standing a moment earlier, but instead to her surprise a young girl with a rucksack on her back stood calmly chewing gum.

'Gee, we've only arrived, and the situation's explosive already! Didn't think our first trip was going to have this effect on things' she laughed.

'You're American'?

'Yeah, guess you can tell'

'Over for the country festival?

'No, just digging up some roots, me and dad, he's over there somewhere, trying to see if he can do anything to help'

'He a doctor?'

'No, just a good man, my dad, we had just booked in, dad went up to his room to unpack while I went to wander around to check the place out, and the next thing, hey presto, our hotel's on fire'!

Gloria smiled, and called her daughter to see what she'd found out about the fire, Glory B reported that there were no casualties but the restaurant and some of the rooms were badly damaged.

The Clarence was an exclusive hotel, about the most expensive in Fundoran and Gloria for all her years of coming to the festival had never set foot in it; not that she wouldn't have liked to have stayed or at least had a drink in it, but her credit union loan would not have allowed for that luxury. Though, there was nothing wrong with The Country House Hotel; Mrs Kelly's personality and her treatment of all her guests in particular, could not be paid for with any amount of money.

The girls had seen enough so now they headed back to their hotel, glad they had unpacked earlier. Gloria would have time for a lie down for an hour or so and Glory B would have time to have a cool pint of soda water and lime before dinner and to see if there were any talent staying in their hotel. As she made her way down the three flights of stairs she wondered if the rest of the week would be as unpredictable as the start!

Chapter six: Fate

Gloria showered then wrapped a towel around her body before choosing what to wear from her suitcase. Glory B decided that the green clingy top and denim mini skirt would show off her mum's fantastic figure 'I'm not too sure about the green' Gloria sighed, 'you know, green for grief!' There was a brief silence before Glory B replied,

'If you've got it, Gloria, you may as well flaunt it!'

Gloria wasn't glamorous as such, but she wasn't plain either; she kept her hair cropped stylishly and mahogany and always wore earrings to match her top. There was a sexiness about her that attracted sometimes unwanted attention from young bucks who thought every woman who wore a low top and short skirt was game for anything.

Gloria's make up consisted routinely of a dash of blusher, black eyeliner carefully applied thinly on the upper eye lid only and always pink lipstick, no matter what she would be wearing, she never changed the colour of her lipstick.

'Gloria, try my red lipstick, go on it'll go better with your top, pink sort of looks daft with green, don't you think?'

'No……. you know I don't care, the colours all match

in my mind, that's all that matters. I don't want to be a Barbie doll!'

'Mum, Barbie's all wear pink! Don't you think?'

'No, I don't think, I'm stubborn, remember, and now don't put me in bad form before we even go out, sweetheart!' Glory B obeyed and combed her hair down keeping the left side behind her ear to show off the crystal earring that sparkled, changing colours as she moved. She wore her lilac lace top, white jeans and 3 inch yellow patient sling-backs. She looked sensational; it was no wonder when she entered a room that all heads would turn. Glory B had a sophisticated beauty; there was an eloquence about her that was unusual for someone so young. She fitted into any company with ease; she could also adapt to most situations; for example, when she met her father for the first time.

Glory B knew very little about her father in fact her mother Gloria also knew very little about him as well, for they had met, went to the cinema, went for a walk in the Falls Park and had sex in his dead grandmother's bed, all within three weeks of meeting and parting. Then 15 years later, Glory B finally met the man whom she was glad had nothing to do with her upbringing.

Bernard was an Australian, his grandmother Maisie O'

Toole was from Leeson Street off the Falls Road in Belfast, his father Vincent, himself an only child, had emigrated to Australia in 1949 where he met and married an Australian called Carol. They had 5 sons and had visited Ireland only once; the occasion being the death of Vincent's mother. Bernard O Toole was a handsome teenager; he had long wavy red hair that he kept tied back and wore Moses sandals with no socks, and really that was all Gloria could remember about him. They met at his grandmother's wake when Gloria was helping to make tea. Neighbours in those days did all they could in providing refreshments and food for the family of a bereaved neighbour. Maybe it was the strangeness of the accent or the mystery it invoked that made Gloria want to know more about, and of course, to comfort this handsome stranger. It was a brief affair and had meant nothing at all to Bernard; but to Gloria it meant much more then and afterwards. At the time things seemed to rollercoaster with such urgency, maybe because of the troubles in Belfast and also because Bernard would be going home to Australia the week after the funeral.

For Gloria, this was her first real romance; the sex was a rushed job in the grandmother's bed the night before Bernard's departure; two strangers from different worlds each looking for something the other couldn't possibly comprehend, and for Bernard, he really wasn't interested in any case. There were no whispered good-byes, nor even a last lingering sensual kiss that Gloria could relive over and over in her mind. She felt used!

Gloria was shocked when 4 weeks later she began to feel quite ill. She hadn't told anyone about what had happened that night because she felt embarrassed and for good reason. How could she explain to her best friend that it happened in Maisie O'Toole's death bed with a boy she'd only met the previous week? How unromantic and even a bit scary, for Gloria couldn't get Maisie out of her mind as she lay naked in the old lady's boudoir. The experience was the complete opposite to what she'd dreamed it would be like. Gloria had always thought that her first time would have taken at least all night with The First Time by Gladys Knight and the Pips softly playing on repeat in the back ground; while, in between the lashings of love, whispers of undying devotion as two bodies finally became one! Instead, afterwards she remembered only the cold and awkwardness as Bernard pushed and shoved to make these two bodies one. She wanted to forget how this handsome young man had coaxed her to take all her clothes off, this was something she was not prepared for that night, for if she had known, she definitely would have bought new knickers for the occasion; she couldn't see him wanting to take her discoloured white bry-nylon briefs back to Australia as a sort of souvenir to drool over when he would recount the experience in his mind!

Glory B was 14 years old when she met Bernard. There was a coldness about him and Glory B was glad she took her outlook on life after her mother. Bernard wanted to bring Glory B back to Australia for a holiday. Glory B declined, though her mum hadn't influenced her one way or the other, it was entirely her own decision. Bernard had known about his daughter 10 years before he came looking. He and his wife had no children so Gloria was suspicious of his sudden interest in Glory B.

He wined and dined his daughter and flashed his money, but Glory B was not easily fooled by his gold or his promises of a better life for her in Australia. It was tempting for Glory B, because she had never known what it was like to have the things that others kids had, but she was an smart child and knew how much she was loved by her mum; that kind of love could never be bought and of course like anyone else who has very little materially, bribery was something to be considered. But Bernard headed back to Australia with a heavy heart, for he had got to know his daughter quite well in those few weeks and for the first time in his life he realised his mistake in walking away all those years ago.

Gloria was an open book, or so everyone thought, but she kept some things to herself that she just could not share with anyone.

Before Bernard came to meet his daughter, Gloria had secretly hoped that maybe there would be a spark, just maybe, but in fact Bernard acted like he was there on a business transaction rather than on a personal journey to embrace his past and bring it into the present and from there onward to an integral part of his future.

Sadly during those three weeks Gloria felt excluded and she would think back to that night in the grandmother's bed and she had ask herself if she had wanted to have sex with him or not, or did he just go too far without her consent. These thoughts had not occurred to her at the time, it was only years later when she had happier and loving relationships, that she understood things a lot better; for then she was a virgin and had no experience of that sort of intimacy; but now, Gloria was comfortable with her body, she was in touch with her inner self and seen her sexuality as a wonderful gift that was given not to be used and dumped but to be mutually enjoyed in any caring relationship she had entered into willingly. She had no hang ups nowadays and enjoyed good sex with men she liked and trusted and who liked her; but she made sure that she was the one who walked away first;

physically at least, emotionally not always!

Into the excitement of the evening the two girls stepped lightly from their hotel armed only with the desire to be sung to by their singing hero Joe Dolan and of course their mobile phones, in silent mode. As they had earlier agreed nothing to do with Gloria's bad news would be mentioned during this week of music, wine and hopefully romance; the thought of which might brighten up Gloria's dark winter evenings. This had to be the best week ever; but a dread dominated Gloria's mind that it may well be her last!

Chapter seven: Old Flame

Joe Dolan was singing in Jury's hotel and the road up to it was chocker blocked. Country fans from every corner of Ireland and further afield walked in procession to their annual pilgrimage to pay homage to their country idols. Gloria was glad she'd wore her white diamond strapped sling backs with the small heels, it made walking a lot easier and safer since last year she went over on her heal and sprained her ankle trying to catch up with Julie, who had coaxed her into wearing the pair of three inch heels.

The atmosphere along the road was jovial; over the years fans became acquainted by sight and although they would seldom meet one another outside of the country music environment, during this week it was like a family get together where fans reminisced about bygone festivals: missing faces, new songs and old favourites. There were good vibes of great expectation from fans who hoped that a young singer by the name of Roco O Neill would top the bill in some of the smaller venues during the week. Roco was from Ballyshannon just a few miles down the road and had made his début last year after being called to the stage by Joe himself; such an endorsement would help build the reputation of any up and coming country star.

Smaller venues were more intimate in many respects because the singer and audience could interact in a more personal way and if you were willing and lucky you might be called to join the singer for a duet; this would be like a dream come true for any country fan.

As the girls queued in the foyer a hand smelling of Old Spice aftershave covered Gloria's eyes and a groggily voice whispered,

'Gee, aint she sweet, from her pretty little head to her feet, Miss Gloria, how are you, doll?'

Cape Canaveral, it can't be, Gloria's mind raced and Glory B stepped back a little to view this insane looking cowboy who possibly was mistaking her mum for someone else. But no, there was no mistake, Gloria knew him well or at least she and her friend Julie both had a close encounter with him a few years back when Chrystal Gale had topped the bill at the festival. They had nicknamed him Cape Canaveral, as in a rocket launcher for obvious reasons; at least they were obvious to Gloria and Julie!

As he turned Gloria around he said in that distinct voice of his,

'You sure look good, where's your honky tonk friend,

Miss Julie'

Gloria remembered that Poncho, yes Poncho (that was what he told them his name was) always put Miss in front of every female he was addressing, like:

'How's Miss Gloria today' or 'oh Miss Julie you'd make any man blush', things like that that soon became boring. Gloria knew she was going to miss Julie more than ever if this rocket launcher Cape Canaveral was going to pester her for this coming week, Julie had an easy going temperament and took the time to get to know everyone even if they were a rocket launcher!

'Who's this gorgeous girl in fresh skin, Miss Gloria?'

Glory B looked mortified and quickly turned away.

'This is my daughter, Glory B' she couldn't avoid being grabbed and kissed as he lifted his cowboy hat momentarily of his head then smiling he flashed a mouth full of gold plated teeth and placed the cowboy hat back where it had proudly sat covering a few strands of well-oiled hairs across their domain of natural baldness; Gloria couldn't keep her face straight as she thought of what Julie would be saying if she were there, it would have been something like 'that's a quire smack of the rubbers, my turn now, please, got to get my ration of passion as well, you know!' Julie could joke her way through anything and at this moment Gloria knew she would miss her so much, yes Glory B was there and that meant a lot, but she couldn't let go with her daughter the way she needed to this week, she could only go that mile with her best friend!

'Gee Pancho, you look good, and you haven't changed a bit since last year! How's the mother and step daddy?' Before he could answer he spotted someone else further down the queue and bolted saying,

'See you both later Miss Glories!'

'Mum, please tell me that was only a friendly kiss; tell me you never, mum, with him please?

Gloria laughed ' look, don't worry I never with him, but something you have to understand, and that is, this week is sort of crazy, we all do things, you know, it's the music, it gets us all carried away with things, I mean, him I'd never but Julie, you know what Julie's like, she'd go with anyone with two legs! That's a fact; I've never heard her turn anyone down!'

'Oh mum you are both worse than I thought'. Glory B whispered that with embarrassment looking round to see if anyone could hear them. Standing behind them was a young girl and an older man obviously old enough to be the girl's father. The young girl was trying to remove something from the man's eye; he was tall and sort of handsome with dark curly hair and conspicuously over dressed for the occasion. His navy pin stripped suit with matching waistcoat and young girl trying to wipe his eye, painted a picture in Glory B's mind of a sugar daddy, she'd never seen one in real life but he looked like the personification of one if ever there was one!

'Don't look now, Gloria, but just behind us is not only a sugar babe but also a sugar daddy, cross my heart, but whatever you do, do not look behind!' Immediately Gloria turned, unable to resist the temptation as Glory B muttered

'May as well talk to myself.......'

Gloria recognised the young girl from earlier in the day at the hotel fire. She had said she was waiting on her dad, so that must be him, the hero who helped tackle the fire. Gloria's mind went into overtime thinking, he wasn't bad looking, but not her type. Though Gloria's type these past two years was sort of non-existent, for outside of an instantly regretted snog with Pancho last year she really didn't have a type per se. She longed to have a type but she couldn't settle for just a little love and a good time the way her friend Julie did. No, there had to be something there, something exciting and mutual before Gloria would indulge nowadays in romance, she had been let down too many times in the past. Her expectations at the start of a relationship would soon evaporate and towards the end she always found that she had been settling for less without realising it; she had a foolish heart but always plenty of hope that one day true love would find her, seek her out and never let her go! She never for one moment thought that it was unrealistic to think that love, mister love, would come knocking on her door, seek her out, ear mark her for his special attention. Maybe mister love was standing no more than a soft breeze from her right now, maybe family roots wasn't all he was looking for either!

Unknown to Gloria, Henry Dickson had eyed her up earlier as she walked in procession towards the hotel. He was fascinated with her wiggle. Gloria had long slender legs and a neat little bum that moved from side to side as she walked. The mini skirt was tight and so it accentuated her hip movement feeding the imagination of hungry men like Henry behind on the road.

Henry was wearing the navy pin stripped suit he had changed into back at The Clarence when the fire was discovered. The rest of his belongings were in the wardrobe and probably destroyed because his room was directly about the kitchen where the fire had started; so he was feeling not only a bit hot but also conscious that he was somewhat overdressed for the occasion. But now at this moment when he noticed Gloria look his way he thought to himself, not bad, quite attractive, like the earrings; he blinked several times as Kelly removed the piece of dirt from his eye and Gloria looked away quickly thinking he was winking at her!

Soon they would be in one another's arms and there would be the opportunity to explain.

Chapter eight:
Let the music begin

The hall was packed and an electrifying atmosphere shot through an already excited grouping of Joe Dolan fans. There was rapturous applause, whistles, shouts and cheers from ecstatic fans as their white-suited star was led on to the stage by an enormous spot-light. Before the crowd even calmed down, like a king adored by his subjects, Joe raised his arms as if to adore them back and burst into a favourite song;

More and More; fans couldn't contain themselves and danced on the spot they occupied.

A surge of adrenalin rushed through Henry's body as the music transformed everything in his being and like a bee looking for someone to lay its sting upon, his eyes frantically searched through the crowed hall and rested on the girl who had made his heart quicken while walking up the road earlier.

Nothing like this had ever happened to Henry before. There was something magical in the music that forced all his dancing inhibitions to exit his usually restrained physique without even a hint of inner coaxing. As the music pounded, so too did both Henry and Gloria's hearts; across the crowed room it suddenly felt that their bodies were destined to be one, and instead of feeling his Irish roots, Henry quite unexpectedly felt somewhere deep within, that he was experiencing Greek roots; for in all his life he had never responded to music in this care free way; but then again he had never heard Joe Dolan sing before. Henry was not an emotional man, he would consider things carefully before making a move, but now, he seemed enchanted as if he were under a hypnotic spell of some sort. Part of the truth was that he had never been to a concert in his life, and so had never had the advantage of letting himself go in this way in public; nor did he usually act on impulse, until this very moment, that from out of nowhere was about to seize him. He wasn't listening to the words, but the beat of the music tuned his heart into something he knew little of.

Gloria was the opposite; she was used to letting go; no inhibitions curtailed her during her annual trip to the festival; though she wasn't an exhibitionist, but she didn't see the point in not going with the flow; and now she was swaying and waving both arms in the air as the words resounded in her head: Gloria always sang her own words to every song:

'More and more and more I want you near me

Time and time again I try to find you

Reaching out my hand I try to touch

I try to feel,

But you're not there you're not real

Time and time again

I try to find you'

And as if she heard the gently call of a lonely heart she turned and through the dancing crowd it was as though a magical path had been made for their eyes alone to meet; the sea of fans had parted enough to enable these two hearts from different worlds to seek and find a kind of solace in the unknown of each; both hearts burned as they were carried towards one another like a pair of birds on the ocean waves casting their fate to the wind; then the dance began............

It was like a scene from a Benny Hill sketch as Gloria, seemingly floated nearer and nearer into Henry's waiting arms, when a collision knocked her flying into the arms of Poncho, the man with the golden teeth! They both fell to the floor and Poncho's hat went up in the air and out of sight. Gloria felt about the floor for the heel of her sling-back shoe; out of nowhere a tall shadow covered her floored body and a hand holding her severed heel calmly spoke in a gentle American accent:

'I'm a dab hand at fixing heels, lady!'

He pulled her quickly back onto her feet; hand in hand they walked toward the door leaving Poncho to get up unaided; annoyed he shouted unheard

'Hey mister, thanks a lot, thanks for nothing, you too Miss Gloria'.

Outside Gloria felt slightly strange, she hadn't the excuse of the magic of the music for leading her astray; no, at this moment she was where she wanted to be and with a man she didn't know but with whom she wanted to be with, alone!

Henry didn't know actually what was going on between himself and this mini-skirted beauty. He thought he should introduce himself before letting go of her hand.

'Hi' his soft American voice sent goose pimples through Gloria's body; she was speechless and just gazed into his hazel eyes,

'You've two different coloured eyes' he smiled

'Obviously, you know that……they're cute, I mean

they're lovely!'

Henry still held Gloria's hand as she searched his face for a flaw, for something to put her off him, something she wouldn't like, but she could find nothing; everything seemed perfect; his smooth tanned skin, his nose, eye lashes, the lot, some face she thought, what does he think of mine,

Neither Kelly nor Glory B noticed their parents had danced off somewhere without them, for they also were sucked into the wave of emotion that flowed through every fan; like a contagious hiccup it was almost an impossibility not to be infected. Both teenagers inhaled the atmospherics of the music and loved every minute of it. It was good for them not to feel under the type of pressure they would normally feel with their own age group, there was something 'cool' about being with an older crowd, though there were many present not too much older than them. Both Kelly and Glory B looked like they had been country fans all their lives, they seemed to know every single word of every song Joe belted out; it wasn't until his first slow song The Answer to everything that the two daughters realised their parent was missing.

The two girls at the same moment made their way over

to the door and out into the foyer, in fact Glory B held the door open for Kelly as she strutted close behind her.

'Pardon me' said Kelly to Glory B and smiling like she was being interviewed for The Rose of Tralee or some other beauty contest;

'Pardon me, but, where are the male toilets? Are there toilets somewhere here ….. or are they outside?'

'This is a hotel not a shack babe, straight across and through the second door'. Glory B hadn't meant to sound sarcastic but that's the way it came out!

'Thanks, sugar….babe' replied Kelly to Glory B's embarrassment; realising that this was the girl with the sugar daddy and she had obviously overheard what Glory B had said to her mum about them, she was left holding open the door open as Kelly strutted off towards the gents; then moving quickly Glory B darted towards the ladies where she thought her mum might had taken refuge.

About 30 seconds later the two girls found themselves back parentless in the foyer. Neither looked at the other as they made their way to the main doors, this time Kelly held open the door and Glory B walked straight through without acknowledging the gesture.

There wasn't as much as a slight breeze to generate some relief as the temperature continued to rise, making stronger the smell of the salted air that hung low about the hotel grounds towering reverently above the Atlantic Ocean. There was no defining line in the distance where the sea and sky met; the blue haze from the ocean formed a bubble and there on top of these ancient rocks both scattered and clustered were lovers and singers and musicians and poets, all with happy or lonely souls, waiting; waiting on its metaphoric circumference to tip them one way or the other, quickening their immediate destiny either soaring them to the limitless sky or lowering them to the depths of the ocean below!

To where would Gloria and Henry freefall through this unexpected encounter? Would their journey together end before it started, maybe, if their daughters had anything to do with it!

It was obvious to anyone who was looking that the man and the woman standing over by the rhododendron, were madly in love; yes madly in love, not just quietly or contentedly in love, for that was the type of love that people of their age were generally regarded to be in. It was the body language that told of the type of love they were in! They stood so close; deliberately not touching; bodies facing each and eyes locked; he breaks the pink head of a rhododendron placing it in her hand, she nestles it to her breast and from a distance it looks like (if you can read lips) she's saying, you broke this beautiful flower without a thought, will you break my heart without a thought also? Never, never, (he might be replying) Then as both daughters shout to distract the love-birds in case they can't reach them before something happens between them but the lovers are oblivious to anything outside of the beat of the others heart; for they are encased in a transparent and delicate bubble that for now protects them from a world of caring teenage daughters.

Chapter nine: Unchain my heart

The two girls looked on as Henry and Gloria walked away through the haze of heat in a daze. What's going on here Kelly thought looking after them; Glory B more or less thought the same. The two girls looked mystified at one another following curiously behind their seemingly besotted parents. Parents who gaze lovingly into the eyes of a stranger, whom they've just met, mind you, cannot be trusted to be alone with the said threat! They need to be safeguarded from such an unhealthy atmosphere that this music seems to have created between them. Luckily for both party's they have daughters who not only love them but will go to any lengths to protect them from 'the danger of a stranger' who might have only one intention in mind and that intention might be dishonourable; from a daughter's perspective!

The situation got worse by the second as both girls in their enthusiasm to rescue their vulnerable parents pushed wide open the two entrance doors to the hall and knocked to the ground two security guards who were standing at the back of each of the doors. To those standing close by it looked like a scuffle had broken out and some big man grabbed both shocked girls by the arms and was escorting them back out through the foyer pursued by the security guards; oblivious to the commotion created in their honour Gloria and Henry danced as all new lovers dance; and in the background Joe sang Unchained Melody; not even the cheers and vibration of banging feet, that called for Joe to sing it again could separate or disturb this new intimacy that clung in harmony between two lonely hearts.

Outside the two girls were trying to explain to the security guards that they were only following their parents back into the hall and didn't realise how light the doors were

'we were rushing for god's sake' Kelly protested,

'my mother was with a stranger, she doesn't even know his name don't you understand, if it was your mother, what would you do, let her wander off with'

Kelly cut in quickly, 'what you saying, my dad's some sort of a …. a knife man or what'

'Well, for all we know, your dad could be ………. anything, I don't know!'

The security men laughed and not missing a chance to chat up two good-looking girls, introduced themselves.

'I'm Bill, and he's Ben' they removed their hats to reveal

two shinning baldy heads and Glory B was almost tempted to ask Bill to bend his head slightly so she could see if her mascara had run!

'You're Bill and you're Ben….. is this some sort of a joke or an Irish chat up line' enquired Kelly.

'Are you brothers or something?'

'Not brothers…..cousins' Ben said with a smile and an accent that Kelly found quite quaint!

'Cousins, who'd have guessed!' deliberate sarcasm entered Kelly's tone; for she was still immature enough to judge people by their looks and neither guard registered on Kelly's good looking scales!

Both girls looked at one another realising that Bill and Ben were seriously trying to pick them up.

'Doing anything later girls?'

'Yes, boys, we've to put mum and dad to bed and tuck them in so they can't wonder after hours' said Kelly nodding for Glory B to confirm. Glory B clicked on right away and nodded in agreement.

'You both sure are good girls to take care of aging parents like that, but what about tomorrow? We're on duty tomorrow night, so maybe tomorrow day we all might get together for a gargle and a bit of craic!'

Kelly stared at Bill as if she'd just seen a ghost. Everyone stared back at Kelly bemused by her wordless reaction; after a few moments of staring at one another, Kelly took a deep swallow and informed the waiting three

'I don't do drugs' then ran as fast as she could in through the foyer and to the safety of the ladies!

Glory B was swiftly in pursuit of this intriguing stranger who one minute had an attitude problem and the next was acting like little girl lost!

The 'ladies' was a lot cooler than outside in the garden; the fan spun round at great speed from the ceiling and made the most annoying humming noise. There was a mirror covering the whole wall facing the door as Glory B entered; she called out as she checked her appearance fixing her earring that had caught on her long dark locks and ran her finger across her lips smoothing the red lipstick that still looked as good as when she'd put it on ages ago. She smiled at herself. ; flashing her white teeth and called out if everything was all right to the closed toilet door. There was a silence followed by a few sobs.

Glory B gently knocked on the toilet door and said, 'Look, come out and tell me what's wrong, come out now before a crowd comes dashing in from the hall!' There was silence. Glory B knocked again. 'Tell me what happened, I didn't get it, come on, there's only me here we're on our own'. Slowly the door opened inwards and at the same moment the outer door banged open and about a dozen women rushed in almost on top of one another singing the chorus of House with the white washed gable: Without a second thought Glory B grabbed Kelly by the hand and ushered her through the stampeding Joe Dolan fans; some pushed their way into the toilets as others stood dancing in front of the mirror swaying and singing: 'I'm in love with the girl who lives in the house with the white washed gable, dum-de-dum, dum-de-dum-de-dum, dum-de-dum-dum-dum' Whatever magic Joe was casting with his songs, all his fans were catching and loving every ounce of it; though to Kelly it seemed more like an epidemic and she began to wonder if they were all on something; her dad included!

The girls sat in the quiet of a shaded bench where a row of pine trees obscured them from the hotel building. It was a spot ideal for lovers or those seeking solitude. On a stormy day the sea below would crash in between the rocks spraying the grass at their feet with its rage; it was hard to imagine the sea in bad form on a day such as this.

The view and the smell of the pines were evocative to both

girls. They sat still, side by side. Kelly taking deep breaths closed her eyes to remember a time in a cabin back home just after Cathy ran off with the gardener. Henry rented a log cabin on top of The Blue Mountain; it was a wonderful place, the mixture of woodland smells encouraged a sense of being separate from the world beyond such a fascinating domain; the soft ground carpeted between the trees with ivy and bluebells that gave a blue sheen visible from miles along the road below. Day and night the smell of pines and the burning log fire that Henry kept going even through the night; in hindsight perhaps the fire was a metaphor for an eternal flame that Henry carried for Teresa his only true love and Kelly's mother.

They didn't see another human being that whole week and barely a word passed between them; the constant sound of the crickets had eventually agitated Kelly and even the birds cooing to one another from high up in the trees had become a source of annoyance; but maybe this was because she felt hurt at her father's lack of trust or faith in her; she wanted him to talk to her, to tell her what he was really thinking and feeling, but he didn't, he couldn't and in a way that week in the Blue mountain had put a distance between them and no matter how much Henry tried on their return home to get close to his daughter it just never happened.

How could he have understand what Kelly was feeling if she didn't tell him for it never occurred to Henry that Kelly, after losing her mother had let Cathy into her world only because she thought her father wanted her to and she wanted him to be happy again. It also never occurred to Henry that Kelly felt betrayed by Cathy's affair and then her leaving them both without a word; she thought he didn't understand that she too had feelings; it seemed to her ten year old mind that her love and understanding had counted for nothing. She felt excluded from her father's internal world.

'What are you thinking about?' Glory B asked; unable to take her eyes of Kelly's flawless skin and eye lashes that were long and curled up without mascara, she even had a long slender nose and lips that looked like they were pumped up; she was so drop dead gorgeous but Glory B felt no envy towards her because she was also drop dead gorgeous, and she knew it!

'Just thinking…… 'Kelly opened her eyes and breathed deeply;

'You can share with me, I don't repeat things, honest, by the way my names Glory B, this isn't exactly my scene either……..I'm here with my mum Gloria, that's she with

the beautiful figure dancing with, your dad, I take it……..
he is your dad, isn't he?'

'Yeah, he's my dad O.K……… this isn't our scene or it
wasn't, looking at dad I don't know now………..we're here
to trace our roots!' Kelly sighed.

'Sounds interesting, we're here, I mean, I'm only here
because Gloria' she said with a smile 'her best friend Julie
didn't come this year, she went to Nashville Tennessee,
they come here every year, they love it…………the whole
thing, the lot, the music the dressing up, the country boys,
they love it all!'

'I thought Gloria was your mum' Kelly said looking
directly into Glory B's eyes.

'She is, we're on first name terms' laughed Glory B.

Kelly looked puzzled but turned away taking more
deep breaths breathing in the smell of the pines and
remembering back as she heard the chirp of a grasshopper
skip somewhere in the long grass behind her.

'What does the smell remind you of?'

Before answering she sighed deeply once more, 'it
reminds me of a ten year old kid who wanted her father to
love her!' she replied with a childlike honesty.

'And did he?'

'He did………….as best as he could, the trouble was the ten year old kid didn't understand that it was his best, she felt rejected, that even he, her dad, was holding back on her. She felt that no one could ever love her, for herself anyway!'

'Sounds like the ten year old kid had a hard time growing up……I suppose she is grown up?'

'You're no dope………….are you!' she smiled looking at Glory B and wondering what age she was!

'So you were an unloved kid at 10?'

'Don't say it like that……my dad's a good guy, a great father, he just had a rough time and I was only a kid; how could I understand what he'd been through!……….and he couldn't understand how I'd been feeling so it was check mate and the sad thing was neither of us knew what the next move should be; emotionally I guess for a while we just drifted apart; I could feel it but I don't think dad did…………..coping with the business seemed to be his priority……….not me!'

'What about your mum, where was she?

Kelly looked out to the sea for a moment before answering. She told Glory B about her mum and also about Cathy. Afterwards she wasn't sure if she really should have shared all this with someone she'd only just met; but she enjoyed talking to someone about her mother and what it had meant to lose her at such a young age.

Glory B enjoyed listening to Kelly's story it felt like they had bonded in some way. Both being an only child and having one parent was something that unique they had in common. Glory B now felt that she knew Kelly well enough to ask about earlier with Bill and Ben.

'It was a bit over the top running off like that, it was only a bit of craic with the boys, do you seriously think I'd be seen dead on a date with either of them!'

'Kelly looking very serious replied 'tell me………… what do you mean by a bit of craic?'

'A bit of craic………fun. What else would it mean?' Glory B seemed to be talking with her hands to Kelly's amusement. A smile broke across Kelly's face and she laughed loudly!

'Hell...craic is fun, like a good time here you mean……………not like drugs at home! Boy, am I crazy!'

'I suppose we've different ways of saying things' Glory B was intrigued and asked why Kelly should have taken the word craic so personal. Without hesitation Kelly told Glory B a lot of things about her addiction and rehab and how she had hurt Henry and now they were getting it together she had promised herself she'd never do anything to bring back that pain on him ever again; it was not easy to tell all this even to a stranger, but by telling it, Kelly felt a kind of release from it all, for there were things she'd never be able to tell Henry, like things she'd done to get money and about people she associated with! If Henry had known the half of it he'd have been so ashamed of her, she told Glory B; but how could she have known that her dad did know all the bad bits but he never once gave up on her. The bond that quickly grew between the two girls was almost tangible by the time Glory B had finished telling her story; particularly the time concerning her dad Bernard O'Toole and the dope incident at school. They both laughed realising that Kelly had earlier referred to Glory B as being no dope!

'Language is a strange thing, don't you think? I think we should always listen and say what we mean and mean what we say!'

'That sounds awfully like one of Gloria's quotes from Muhammad Ali, don't tell me you're into boxing'

'Muhammad Ali, who's that, should I know him!' They both fell about laughing.

Kelly had arrived in Ireland a few hours ago a lonely soul, in search of something deeper than her Irish roots and now out of nowhere she had found her perfect soul mate. From a distance it looked like the girls had known one another all their lives, the body language between them was easy and comfortable; their friendship was sealed as they made their way inside the dance hall to see what the lovebirds were up to now!

Chapter ten: Teresa

If there had been a bomb warning Henry would have danced on. He saw no one except this beautiful woman he held in his arms. If there had been an earth quake Gloria would have let it swallow her up; she would not have run away from the feeling that Henry's two strong arms gave her.

The past week and the years before had all disappeared, melted away as their bodies understood they were now where they belonged; it was like coming home at last after being lost in a desert. They were comfortable together and if either believed in reincarnation then that could account for why they should feel the way they did about each other. Could they have been lovers in a former life? Something familiar to each was triggered as they gazed into the others eyes.

The show was breaking for 15 minutes; the lights went up and everyone stopped dancing, except for Gloria and Henry.

'I'm Henry' he whispered in her ear

'and I'm yours' she whispered in a seductive tone

'you smell delicious' he said still softly

'you smell of fire………got a spare light' she winked; they both laughed and still oblivious to anyone else in the hall they kissed…………the two daughters hurried across the floor like two arresting marshals calling the offenders by name in a vain attempt to distract the courting couple before the kiss got too heavy.

'Good god dad, what are you doing?' snarled Kelly.

Both girls waited on a reply or some sort of acknowledgement that they were there.

'Gloria…… back to the hotel, right now, come on, you're embarrassing me, come on, please don't make a scene!' Glory B commanded in an unconvincing voice!

Gloria and Henry sort of laughed at the idea of their children scolding them for their behaviour; Henry held onto Gloria's hand and squeezed it gently. Henry smiling and Gloria giggling were led outside by the arresting marshals.

Henry remembered this feeling of being caught on many years before. It was a November night in a time when kissing in the dark was all a boy could hope for going out with a catholic girl; however, this night the teenage sweethearts, Henry and Teresa, consumed with passion as they listened to Elvis sing 'It now or never'; they were true Elvis fans and Henry had saved his paper round money to buy this poignant song for Teresa to play on her new portable record player; they had the house to themselves and in tune with Elvis singing my love won't wait Henry whispered deeply into Teresa's sensitive ear those words of eternal love as his young lively body pressed tightly onto Teresa's; such a beautiful moment that end so badly.

Teresa's parents came home to a darkened house, the living room door banged opened, the lights switched on and a scream rang out! It was Teresa's mum almost hysterical finding Henry on top of her innocent daughter on the settee. Although they were only kissing, startled and frightened for his life, Henry fall back ways onto the floor with Teresa on top of him. He was escorted to the hall door by Mick, Teresa's dad, who was usually an easygoing fellow; Henry had never seen him in such a rage before. Teresa ran crying upstairs to her room. All that night Henry felt confused and irritated, he made up his mind that he and Teresa would get married as soon as they were of age! And they did!

Now, a flood gate of memories open and gushes through

Henry's mind; but, putting them to the side he smiles acknowledging to himself that his beautiful daughter is truly at home with him in his heart! Father and daughter once more.

Indoors was too hot for the girls so they decided to walk back to into town to check out the beach, leaving their parents with a stern warning not to do anything they wouldn't do themselves, in public at least! As Glory B switched on her mobile 3 new messages came through. They were all from Julie asking where Gloria was and to get her to switch on her mobile that it was an emergency – life or death!

'It's Julie trying to get Gloria, probably to tell her about the latest man she's picked up……..honestly they're like two kids the way they get on!'

'Don't you want to go back and tell your mum in case it's important, maybe she's in trouble or something?'

'No, Julie's always got trouble…..man trouble!' they laughed and walked down the winding pathway impervious to Julie's cry for help! As they crossed from one side of the road to the other a red van driven by Rico O Neill came screeching towards them making them both jump out of its way! Kelly shouted after the driver

'You son of a bitch………rot in hell! Kelly helped Glory B up she wasn't hurt but her white jeans were badly marked and the heel of her yellow patient sling -back was lying in the middle of the road. They gave the beach a miss and instead went back to the hotel where Glory B got changed and then went for something to eat. There was plenty of choice along the main street of Fundoran but the girls decided on burgers and chips. Everywhere they walked heads turned and boys whistled after them. Neither appeared to be impressed by all this attention, but secretly they enjoyed it!

Back on the dance floor Gloria quickly learned that Henry wasn't much of a jiver, in fact it could be said that he had two left feet and his timing was all wrong he was throwing her round when he should have been pulling her in; Gloria took her jiving seriously as did her friend Julie; usually they took to the floor before anyone else and were considered to be such excellent jivers that only the best of jivers would interrupt the pair to dance with them; no messers would be tolerated! When Joe finished You're Such A Good Looking Woman and the cheers rang out, the band prepared for another slow number. Gloria whispered again seductively into Henry's ear:

'You need lessons on your……… jiving technique'

'You need to teach me……….your technique'

'I could give you some lessons………..private lessons!' Their eyes kissed and the world stood still as the music complimented the flow of unspoken words and once more Gloria fell into the waiting arms of her American stranger! The moment was short lived. That next song was called Teresa. Henry was enjoying this feeling of being with someone after years of being on his own. The softness of Gloria's breasts pressing so gently against his chest and moving to the beat of his heart, was like being a boy again, he felt a surge of anticipation for deep intimacy when suddenly he became aware of the lyrics of Joe's song. He'd never heard the song before otherwise he would have remembered;

'I think I've seen that look before some where I can't be sure – Teresa'

Henry stopped dead, it took Gloria a few seconds to realise that they were not dancing; 'I'm sorry Gloria, I've got to go, got to get back to the hotel.'

'What! ……..you can't be serious!'

'Sorry……..I'll explain later!' And within a moment he was heading for the main doors, alone!

Gloria was mystified, in a daze, until she spotted Pancho move in her direction and she also made a run for it towards the doors!

She caught sight of Henry moving behind the pine trees and she quickly followed. Her mobile alerted her to 6 messages; she switched on to find they were all from Julie, but she had no time to waste on what would probably be Julie's boasts about the men and music in Nashville, for she was caught up in something real and if her instincts were right something good, in her own life!

She found Henry sitting where their daughters' had sat and bonded not so long before; would the vastness of the sea, the full moon that hung in the sky before them, the smell of pines and the solitude of this spot encourage in them a freedom to be honest, for they were not teenagers, they were adults who felt perhaps a little uncomfortable with new feelings about their feelings!

'I don't normally do this'

'Do what' Henry said looking into Gloria's eyes

'Run after a man.........I was really running away from one, you know your man you rescued me from earlier.........well he was about too.....'

Henry put his arm around Gloria, he whispered that he was sorry that he wasn't sure what had come over him, and then he told her his story about losing his wife Teresa and how he'd jumped into a relationship shortly afterwards for the wrong reasons and how it all ended. But, as he explained, that the song Teresa had triggered buried emotions there on the dance floor. He just needed space. It was nothing personal. Gloria felt Henry's cheek and as they're lips were about to meet, her mobile rang to the tune of Honky tong Angel.

'Blasted phone, I bet its Julie again!'

'Nice tune……..could it be important?'

'No, definitely not... it will be about some guy she's picked up'

The phone went dead; Gloria checked her texts and they all were from Julie saying the same in capital letters: HELP. Gloria laughed and thought to herself how typical it was of Julie's bad timing in everything; in fact she'd bad timing down to a fine art and perfected with practice; of course Julie hadn't a clue that she was so good at it! The most memorable and embarrassing occasion of her bad timing was when Gloria was going to tell Eddie Fisher that it was over between them. They went to the cinema; the plan being to tell him afterwards and Gloria would meet Julie in the Mojo bar to tell her the ins and outs of how he took it; but, as fate had it, Eddie said his brother Simon was looking forward to having a drink with them in the Mojo after the cinema. Gloria text Julie explaining the situation but Julie was already in the bar and her mobile was out of credit! As Julie waited she got friendly with someone waiting on his brother and girlfriend, she told him how her best friend was giving her boyfriend the push; bad breath, smelly feet and not a good kisser either, was the description Julie had just finished painting, when entered the unsuspecting couple and the rest as they say was; not a pretty sight!

They resumed where they had left off; the moment had not been lost but enriched by the wait. Without closing their eyes they kissed and it was a soft kiss; a promise of a kiss in waiting; and an interesting kiss if there is such a kiss! They kissed not with passion but with measured short gentle kisses that lovers who know the others thoughts intimately sometimes share; Gloria and Henry were unhurried by time and passion. Everything about this night felt unique. Wonderful! It wasn't until Gloria fell into bed that she remembered the doctor's words! All through the night those words were like a record being played on repeat; and she couldn't switch it off!

Henry and Kelly were sharing a double room at Madden's B&B and it was unlikely they could have separate rooms until the festival was over. Henry wondered if the other guests from The Clarence had been placed in better accommodations than they had! But at least they'd come to no harm even though they had only, for the moment, the clothes they were wearing when the fire started. The up side to today was that Kelly had met Glory B and Henry had met Gloria. And now, it was good night for both exhausted travellers who had found themselves in this new environment with renewed hopes for the future.

'Here you are dad'……..reaching her hand across from her single bed to Henry's double.

'What's this?'

'Just a reminder of today……….' it was her Walkman and a CD of Joe Dolan's greatest hits. 'Thought you might enjoy tasting what you're letting yourself in for!'

The lights went out and they both closed their eyes to the darkness of the room!

Chapter eleven:
Keep reminding me

'Keep reminding me of the promise we made yesterday'? She said with a tinge of desperation pulling a new pink top over her head; she sat on the edge of the bed glancing into the mirror her daughter stood in front of getting herself ready for the day.

'Why? What's going on? Are you feeling frightened........ do you want to go home? We can go now if this is all too much for you!'

'No, I'm just afraid in case I let it spoil things this week, I need to be strong, and I need you to help me be strong..........now enough of this talk, what are we going to do today?'

'Well, I'm meeting Kelly at eleven and we're going to check the beach out........what about Henry, you didn't say much last night not like Gloria to be out of words!' Glory B tied a black bandana round her head and began applying sun block to her face.

'I really like him...........I can't explain it but there's something there between us..........It may come to nothing but it's there, just my luck……….meeting what could be the love of my life the same day as being told I have a brain tumour.'

Glory B handed her mum the sun block to rub on her back as she sat on the bed beside her 'Did you tell him………'

'what do you think……..he'd have felt sorry for me and then run a mile, whatever way the next few days ago, I don't want him to know, so please………princess don't say anything to Kelly'

'I didn't and I wouldn't it's up to you……..my beautiful mum who you want to tell……….I almost forgot, Julie was trying to contact you last night, have you told her?'

'Couldn't get her, mobile switched off as usual when she's got a man, I'll give her a quick call now'.

'Why don't you wait till after breakfast?'

Gloria didn't really feel like talking to Julie so she agreed

'Fine, by the way, we're having breakfast with Henry and Kelly is that o.k. with you?'

'Fine, for you and Henry, Kelly and I don't eat in the mornings but we'll go along for the education of it!' she teased.

'What exactly would you both be getting educated on?' Gloria smiled to herself.

'Well you never know, mother dear….. maybe the facts of life? You know like when a man meets a woman etc. etc.!' She blinked her eyes like a child, whose mother was trying to convince her that Santa Clause was real, when she knew the truth but was pretending she didn't know just to please her mother.

Madden's B&B was a few doors away from The Country House Hotel and Kelly was up like a lark and away shopping for some new clothes for Henry and herself; they could find out about their suitcases later; hopefully their belongings would be undamaged, but for now they needed a few outfits to tide them over and Kelly was making sure that she would chose Henry's clothes and he would have no choice but to wear them.

At home Henry never dressed casual, Kelly couldn't remember ever seeing him wearing a T shirt and jeans, not once and even in the blistering summers of Boston he still dressed himself in shirt, tie and laced up shoes. Kelly was surprised at Henry's reaction to his new outfits. He seemed pleased with his daughter's choice. Looking at himself in the mirror he wondered if Gloria would appreciate his new look; but then Gloria didn't know that it was a new look for they'd only met yesterday and as far as she knew he was wearing the suit because his clothes were still in The Clarence.

'Breakfast at Tiffany's for us this morning'

'You know I don't do breakfast..........I'm meeting Glory B and we're going out hunting'

'Hunting?'

'Yeah..........hunting...........the local talent on the beach!

'Oh I get it.......but be careful....you know what I mean........I might hire a car later and drive over to Ballyshannon to the local church and begin our search for the O'Neill's there!' Kelly felt excited at the prospects of finding her ancestors or at least finding out about them; she had given it a lot of thought since rehab and hoped that it might help her understand better the darker side of her nature that she was finding hard to except. On the surface Kelly seemed detached and uncaring with an air of self-assurance that protected her vulnerability but stopped others from wanting to be friends with her. That profile was the complete opposite to what the real Kelly was like.

'Breakfast at Tiffany's it is then, come on I've a date and can't be late........' he joked and seemed in exceptionally good form. Kelly thought if he was this happy after one day what would he be like after a week in Gloria's company; but this new relationship was not without risk; for both father and daughter. Kelly hoped that it wouldn't be another Cathy affair.

Gloria sat at the window table in Tiffany's Café, so named by a Audrey Hepburn fan as Julie had discovered a few years before when she tried to touch for the then owner, Marcos, a Greek Cypriot who offered Julie a summer job doing the breakfast shift, which she declined on hearing that Marcos had 15 children at home in Nicosia; he also had a wife and a string of cousins; but they had a good time and Marcos thought Julie was hilarious, they even exchanged Christmas cards that year but the following year a new owner had taken the place over and didn't want to talk about Marcos so they never found out what had happened to him; it all sounded a bit mysterious!

Henry looked different today as Gloria watched him cross the road, he suited the navy T shirt and jeans, and he had a good physique: broad shoulders big enough to balance both side of his body beautifully, no beer belly or flab hanging from anywhere; handsome and fit Gloria smiled thinking, just my type! 'Slight change of plan, girls won't be eating breakfast with us, we met Glory B at the post office and she says she'll see you later……..gone hunting I believe' He sat down and they looked at one another thinking secret thoughts that were disturbed by the waitress wanting to take their order.

'Coffee and dry toast for the lady, and you sir, full Irish with pot of tea anything else' she asked with an experienced voice of a woman who knew how to handle customers in a charming way.

'Give me a shout if you need more tea, sir, or coffee'

'Thank you, we'll let you know if we need anything' he winked at the waitress and for a brief second Gloria felt slightly uncomfortable' it was silly really to feel uncomfortable over a wink especially as she didn't know Henry's usual form. Maybe he winks at every waitress who serves him; maybe he just…….. winks, she thought without showing her discomfort.

Henry insisted on paying for breakfast and as he stood up from the table Gloria handed him a bag. 'For you…. hope you like it!'

He took it and before opening the bag he winked at Gloria making her feel warm inside; but it looked like the same wink he gave to the waitress a short time before. Gloria felt confused. His winking was sending out conflicting messages to Gloria.

'There now, you're a proper honky-tonk man' she joked fixing the cowboy hat on his head, he showed no resistance and enjoyed the moment like a school boy wearing his uniform for his first day at school; he could feel that a new chapter was about to begin!

It was mid-day and the beach was crammed with visitors from everywhere; there didn't seem to be anywhere left on the beach to lay a towel and sunbathe but that wasn't the plan the girls had in mind in any case. Barefooted they walked along the water edge up towards the camp site; they were bombarded with wolf whistles but they pretended not to hear as the scorching sand forced them to put their sandals back on; they giggled and hopped across to the camp-site. If they had been mermaids that had swum ashore they could not have been more noticeable because they were both so young and beautiful. From the wooden steps up to the site Kelly noticed a red van which looked identical to the one that almost rammed them the previous evening; standing outside the van was a tall ginger haired young man with arms folded talking to a man and woman who turned out to be Gloria's friends from yesterday, Jean and Sam!

Kelly didn't delay in her attack; she rushed up to Rico O Neill and confronted him directly.

'You son of a bitch, who the hell do you think you are, you almost killed us yesterday!'

Rico remembered the incident although he instantly denied it.

'You look in pretty good shape for someone who I almost killed yesterday………… kid'. The word kid unleashed in Kelly a serious of expletives; Glory B was a bit shocked, Jean just stared as Sam looked away but Rico laughed.

'You're too good looking to come off with garbage like that; it takes away from your good looks…… I'm heading up town shortly; we could meet up for a swally and a bit of craic.

As Kelly stormed off Glory B followed and Jean shouted after her to tell her mum she was asking for her.

Kelly was like someone doing a marathon but finally Glory B caught up with her as she took the wrong turning into the main street and instead ended up at the gates of the parish chapel.

Both girls looked surprised to see two familiar figures accompanied by a priest walking towards them.

'Good God, no………what's this about' Glory B said to Kelly who at this stage was inhaling deep breaths in an effort to calm herself down from the encounter with Rico O Neill!

'Father Hanna, this is Kelly, my daughter'

'and this is my daughter, Glory B' the pleasant mannered priest smiled and shook hands with the girls as Henry explained to Kelly that Father Hanna was in touch with the parish priest in Ballyshannon who was able to confirm that the O'Neill's still lived there and he would give them Henry's mobile number to get in touch. This changed Kelly's mood and she hugged her father saying how exciting this was going to be!

As they walked back towards the beach Gloria's mobile bleeped, it was another text message from Julie, it read, H E L P XO; Gloria ignored this new message for a while then curiosity got the better of her and also for once she did feel slightly concerned.

'Julie, it's me Gloria, what's wrong'... there was a uncanny silence....

'Hi, my name's Sandy, a lady chasing a bus and eating breakfast dropped this here cell phone, I've just picked it up' said a man with an American accent.

'Did she seem all right, by the way where exactly are you

in Nashville?'

'Sorry, did you say Nashville………….this here's Las Vegas lady……….I'll give this here phone to Mr Yansan, he owns the motel your friend was staying at, she can pick it up later mam ……. You still there mam... hope your friend gets it when she comes back…take my word lady, I'm handing it to Mr Yansan in person, bye lady!'

'That's got to be a mistake………someone's pulling my leg……… Julie's put that man up to it'

'Up to what...What did he say Gloria?' There was a hint of concern in Gloria's voice as she read the text message again.

'Whoever that was said he was in Vegas…..Las Vegas'

'Vegas……….are you sure about that' Henry said coolly lifting his right eyebrow like a question mark and smiling into Gloria's eyes.

'That's what the man said, Vegas…Las Vegas'

'Vegas is a long way from Nashville!'

Shaking her head from side to side Gloria replied 'I could write a book about Julie………….nothing surprises me……….I wouldn't be surprised if she rang from the moon!'

Henry bought everyone ice cream from the van at the gates of the camp site, the four strolled along amid country music being played from almost every caravan and tent on the site. There was no sign of the red van or the son of a bitch who drove it and Kelly was relieved because she didn't want to explain to Henry, she could deal with this herself. The atmosphere was different to anything Henry had ever experienced before and he was loving it. The girls went back to the beach while Henry and Gloria sat on a felled tree outside Jean and Sam's tent enjoying the session of country music that was now in full swing. Henry looked the part in his cowboy hat and he wasn't even self-conscious about wearing it!

'What's your kind of music, I mean what turns you on…. musically?' Gloria smiled searching Henry's eyes for a glint of recognition that she really wasn't asking him about his musical taste!

'Well'…. he gave her that wink that melted her defences; she thought she was being careful not to portray how much Henry turned her on but then totally out of character, she blushed. It was a beautiful blush and Henry enjoyed it. He told her it was years from he's caused anyone to blush and it made him feel that he was being quite intimate with Gloria. He felt good inside; though Gloria felt that her blush had given too much away!

Although the moment was gone and Gloria's face was back to its normal colour, still something private had happened between them, something that words alone could not articulate. It was magic!

Henry's taste in music nowadays was a little bit of everything: rock: Elvis of course, heavy metal (Bat out of Hell) John Denver and very recently, The Beautiful South. A little bit of most styles of music really, but no more than a little! He admitted that he had no passion for music the way Gloria had; his admission was sort of like a confession for in this present environment it seemed to Henry that it was a fault not to be crazy about Country Music. He had to tread carefully least he might give a boring impression of himself, putting Gloria off him, in a romantic sense.

Loneliness at bed time had given him a hunger for the written word, mainly the poetry of Shakespeare, Frost, Donne and others, the metaphysical in particular. He reluctantly shared this with Gloria, minus the part about his lonely bedtime ritual, hoping she might understand that he was a man of quiet routine and deep thought.

'Maybe later you'll recite your favourite poem for me….. when we're alone' she teased.

'I only know all the words of one poem by heart, the rest I'd have to read from the book, I didn't think I'd be needing books on this trip, and I hope that stays true till it's over' he replied in a serious tone. Till it's over; those words registered in Gloria's mind with more than a fatalistic connotation about them; her mobile bleeped and any notion of doom quickly passed as she received a blank text from a withheld number.

The one poem Henry knew by heart was the one he said at Teresa's open grave, the day of her funeral. He could never say those words out loud ever again, they were just so precious to him, even sacred, like a new dawn shared with someone, it can never be repeated; you might welcome a thousand dawns but each one is different; each dawn promises unique hope for the day ahead, then it fades and is gone forever, like a stream that runs into a river and then they become one travelling forward now as one and meeting the sea where it is swallowed up and becomes part of a greater plan, it can't be held back. Henry viewed life like a journey, through which the heart and soul travel many diverse roads before meeting up with their finial destiny!

The poem still meant as much now as it did then all those years ago, the words still had the same effect on Henry. Teresa had loved anything written by Christina Rossetti. But now sitting in this fantasy-like atmosphere where earthy smells filtered like drugs through the songs and music delicately intoxicating the gathering of soul hungry listeners who all seemed to Henry to be where they wanted to be at this moment in their lives; he wondered if there was such a terminology known as a unified comfort zone; perhaps this was only how he imagined they looked, but none of them looked out of place, they seemed at ease with themselves. Then Henry heard above the music, birds cooing at one another from their omniscient perches, wings flapping in glorious displays as they moved from tree to tree, the chirp of the grasshopper whose home human feet were trespassing upon; all the inner cities of ants and birds that existed here in the woods Henry was conscious of, but, the musicians and singers, he wondered if they also could hear that other music being played!

If anyone noticed Henry as he sat next to Gloria, it may have seemed like he was lost somewhere deep in the music; who could have known that resounding in his head were those haunting words of Christina Rossetti. Henry closed his eyes and the words with Teresa's voice just fell from the sky:

Remember me when I am gone away, gone far away into the silent land; when you can no more hold me by the hand, nor I half turn to go yet turning stay. Remember me when no more day by day you tell me of our future that you planned; only remember me; you understand it will be late to counsel then or pray. Yet if you should forget me for a while and afterwards remember, do no grieve: for if the darkness and corruption leave a vestige of the thoughts that once I had, better by far you should forget and smile than that you should remember and be sad.

Henry opened his eyes and a good feeling came over him. It was like for some unknown reason he had Teresa's approval to connect with Gloria without reproaching himself for having real feelings for her. He looked at Gloria singing her heart out and he did a most uncharacteristic thing; he consciously began swaying and taping his feet to the sweet, sweet music that was carrying him to a good place within himself. And Henry Dickson felt happy. Really happy!

Chapter Twelve: A New Tune

The girls decided to check out Nellie's, a youngish bar at the far end of Main Street, for tonight. The great Rico O Neill was billed there as the fabulous new Gareth Brooks of Ballyshannon. They both were looking forward to sampling the younger country set. If Glory B had been on her own with her mum, then the whole of the country scene would have been fine, but, because she had teamed up with Kelly and her mum was with Henry, that left them both free to enjoy their own thing!

Glory B, underneath all the cool exterior that oozed from her controlled and appealing nature, was feeling a sadness and vulnerability that she was concealing well. She made a deal with her mum to enjoy this week and not to think beyond until they reached home, where the cruel reality of Gloria's brain tumour awaited them. She felt guilty because she was enjoying the fun that having a carefree friend like Kelly was bringing. She wondered what Kelly would think if she knew the truth about the secret her new friend was carrying. It wouldn't be fair to share this burden with Kelly anyway because, she was here to have a good time and Glory B and her mother would be out of their lives forever by next week. It would be nice to think that this week would turn out to be a wonderful memory for them all; but only a memory; holiday friendships never last, in Glory B experience anyway!

Kelly had learned the value of being true to oneself during her spell in rehab; but also to be realistic about what she expected of others. Because Glory B knew about Kelly's recent past it did not make her her keeper, it was up to Kelly to deal with temptation should any arise; she was feeling strong and confident about steering herself away from any tell-tale signs of dope or anything stronger within the company here in Nellie's. It was entertainment itself being chatted up by a bunch of good looking guys who all seemed keen on both girls and they could have had their pick of any of them if either gave any sign of encouragement.   Kelly felt no need to explain why she didn't drink as she turned down several offers of alcohol; she said she preferred stilled water and this added to Glory B's admiration of her new friend. One of the guys took a fancy to Kelly, his name was Peter and he arranged to meet both girls later in the tiny function room at the back of Nellie's where he would be backing Rico O Neill on the fiddle. Maybe they would make a foursome he jested to

Glory B in a fashion that seemed to be a striking trait in any of the Donegal guys they'd met so far.

Both girls were lapping all the attention up and in response were each unconsciously acting out their own unique diva role to the fascination of their string of admirers; both revelling in every moment of it. A constant stream of young men all entranced by the natural beauty and approachability of both girls hadn't yet tired of trying their luck by asking if they could meet up later. Though the girls didn't have an agenda they decided to go with the musicians, because that almost guaranteed them interesting company and a party into the small hours of the morning. Peter walked them back to their hotels and they made arrangements for meeting up later, they both needed time to wash their hair and shower before hitting the night scene in the busy and buzzing town of Fundoran!

Henry arrived ten minutes early and got talking to Mrs Kelly about Fundoran and what it was like living there off season. She told him how she used the winter months to concentrate on her writing; she wrote songs and performed them in her lounge to the locals who she thought were pretty good judges of talent and if they gave her the thumbs up then she would send the songs to agents that had been recommended to her by passing entertainers; but as yet, nothing had come of anything she'd composed. She asked Henry if he knew anyone in the music business in Boston and he told her he didn't. That wasn't strictly true; he had met Dave James who ran a large recording company in Philadelphia a few months ago and they had much in common. Dave's young daughter Winter, was in rehab the same time as Kelly; both men bonded, and were able to talk openly to one another about what was happening with their daughters. But Henry wasn't prepared to go there for anyone. It's like an unwritten code of ethics, that when you meet someone at rehab unless you knew them before, you never ever mention their name or anything about them to anyone; within the rehab environment people share their experiences but you sometimes get to know things about people, patients and their visitors, that they may share and trust you with because obviously you're in the same boat; but if you were to mention to someone that you know some big shot then it's only natural they'll want to know how you know them. Now, a white lie was sufficient to avoid having to explain anything to anyone that might later lead to having to tell a bigger lie to protect the vulnerable.   Mrs Kelly had charisma and was the type of woman to whom you would confide in, especially after having a one to one with her. Henry liked her and she seemed to be both straight forward and engaging; although this was the first time they'd met he felt he'd known her forever; like some interesting aunt who came to visit occasionally and for whom he felt a fondness; but she was someone he wouldn't be confiding in this time around, at least!

Gloria wore a white lacy top with a red bra underneath and matching red shorts. She looked sensational; Henry's heart skipped quite a few beats as he watched her from the reception desk, glide down the stairs.

'We're having a bit of a hooley here later……will we see you both back before the night's out?'

Henry winked at Mrs Kelly 'Sure you will……see you all later'

Mrs Kelly gave Henry one of her renowned mischievous smiles as she winked back and bide them an enjoyable evening.

The street outside was crowded with fans all making their way up towards the Big Tent which was the place to be tonight; there were three top acts from Nashville and a variety of others from this side of the ocean including

Joe; so, it was not to be missed. They walked hand in hand until suddenly they realised, they were on their own. The fans that had crammed the street below had disappeared and Henry and Gloria were walking beside the river. They had been so engrossed in conversation that neither had noticed taking a left fork up towards where the river was, separating themselves from everyone else. Each wondered to themselves how this had happened. Neither had ever experienced anything so peculiar before; maybe it was the heat of the evening that led them to a cooler quieter space or some untapped rhythm in them drawing them to the gentle movement of the river; like adult children to a mother's breast!

They came upon a large rock that had a flattish top and Henry wondered if it was a mass rock; his father told him about how people in Ireland had to hear mass in secret because the mass was outlawed by the British and a priest would be arrested if he was caught celebrating it. Henry fondly remembered when he was around five or six being tucked up in bed by his father, the nightly ritual seldom changed: night prayers and then a story, usually about Donegal and the length of which depended on what was going on down stairs. Henry had thought the stories about the penal times were only stories that his father made up to encourage him to appreciate mass on a Sunday; he missed the stories when his father died, but he learned much later at school that the stories were true and Henry had even romanced the idea of becoming a priest - until he met Teresa!

To Gloria the rock stood out like a bus stop and was in a perfect spot for anyone seeking a bit of solitude and rest by the river.   All around were discarded butt ends that hadn't quite reached the clean, giggling river and the different cans and bottles were evidence that this was a popular spot for the more inclined nature lovers! Gloria was glad she'd taken her anti-histamine, though she hadn't envisaged being in the midst of such a pollinated area. Henry picked a bunch of blue bells and presented them to her on one knee. They laughed and fooled around as the music from the Big Tent swept through them adding to the sheer bliss of this timeless capsule that had captured their heart. They laughed so much that even the birds remained silent as they gathered in the bushes across, scores of them, many from different flocks perching side by side watching and waiting. Some of the smaller birds made way for two wood pigeons that arrived together; all was well in the bushes until the arrival of one great magpie, it tried to wedge its way in between a row of sparrows; one tiny sparrow took exception to being pushed around and landed the magpie a head on stab with the tip of its beak, the stab was enough to provoke retaliation from another magpie who had just flown across from a great oak further up the river. Now unsettled, the scores of birds flew down stream to find a more contemplative spot and rest their weary wings for the night.

Henry lifted Gloria in his arms and swung her round pretending to throw her into the river. She screamed with excitement throwing her legs in the air and her hands clasped tightly around his neck, and accidentally dropping the blue bells into the water. Henry stopped and they both watched as the flowers separated and were carried away until they were out of sight. Were those wild flowers a euphemism for what was happening between them; they both felt as though they were being swept away on a tide of emotion; would they go their separate ways after this week? Henry's mind was racing, how could he let go of this moment without saying something; he knew he couldn't, for he felt that he was falling in love!

Looking into one another's eyes was like reaching deep down into the others soul, searching for that emotional click so they'd recognise that they had finally both arrived at the same moment in time, their time! Setting Gloria on the edge of the flat rock he stroked her face and pulled her body as close as was possible to his. Gloria wrapped her legs around Henry's waist and they both hesitated momentary to savour the moment; that wonderful moment of decision when there is nothing more honest between two people than the true expression of their feelings for one another! And then they kissed.

The first star of the evening appeared in a low sky and Henry told Gloria to make a wish on it; she closed her eyes and held his hand tightly wishing that this night would never end; and although it would end, it was about to be extended, at least!

'Do you know what that star is called?'

'No……….you tell me…….I want to know everything you know'

'It's called the North Star'

'Really ……..very interesting'

'You're my star……….my northern star!

'That's corny………I don't want to be your Northern Star….that's something you can never have.'

'O.K. then, you're my Northern Rose!'

They both laughed..........'I like that........I like the idea of being earthy, real, touchable........fragile'

'Why fragile?' he puzzled.

'Because I can sense that you're sensitive, and if I'm fragile then you'll always handle me with care! They laughed and danced to the sound of Joe thumping out More and More. Their hearts thumped wildly to the beat of the distant drums and the grasshoppers chirped from behind in the long blades; even the slumbering trout wakened and danced gracefully in and out of the water; everything perfectly in tune.

Time passed so quickly and now it was late and they decided to head back to see how the girls were; their pathway was lit up by countless stars the likes of which Gloria only ever witnessed in Fundoran; the moon appeared to be almost on top of the rocky hills that were flung across the outskirts of Fundoran inspiring Gloria to ask Henry if he too could sense a feeling of being part of the universe, important components even? It was as though the universe's umbilical cord still connected to everything that breathes on planet earth, nurturing the unseen in every molecule around them, and it truly felt like this night belonged to them alone, and the meaning to their lives was unfolding somewhere deep between the seen and the unseen, articulating itself through their emotions. She wasn't sure if he understood what she was trying to explain, but he said he did and that he'd never forget this night, ever! There was still music in the air as they strolled hand in hand towards the moon; but the real music for Henry and Gloria was in their hearts and the beat thumped to a new song that only they could hear.

Chapter 13:
What The Heart Doesn't Know ....

Kelly had thought to herself that the bottled water she was drinking wasn't quite like the Boston bottled water she preferred, but thought no more of it and downed another afterwards. Nellie's was packed to the door and people were bumping into one another if they moved at all. The girls were lucky to get a table up beside the tiny stage. Peter was a lovely guy and very polite but Rico was so self-assured and in love with himself that they seemed an unlikely team. Rico sort of apologised to Kelly for his behaviour at the camp-site but insisted it wasn't him driving the van that almost ran them both over. 'Fine' said Kelly eyeballing him as soon as Peter introduced them, 'at least now I know that you're a liar, a son of a bitch liar'!

'What's your problem.......kid?'

Glory B thought for one horrible second that Kelly was going to bang him across the face.....but thankfully she didn't and Peter put his arm around her and laughed telling them both to relax and enjoy the evening. They had got off to a bad start but Kelly quickly realised that Glory B and Rico were eyeing one another up and down;

she wasn't going to spoil the evening for Glory B just to get her own back on this probable son of a bitch. She was quite capable of waiting until the time was right and they were alone. She was only going to be in Fundoran for a short time so she might as well make the most of it; but tomorrow would be different for she was certain that she would be meeting her long lost relations; and if Peter was still around then maybe that would be a bonus!

For most of the evening the girls had a great time; they enjoyed dancing at their table and giving sexy glances to Rico and Peter who in turn seemed to be singing every song to the girls for they had eyes for no one else in the pub. One fellow kept bumping into Kelly, at first he appeared to be really drunk but Kelly just didn't like something about him, he kept trying to pull Kelly up to dance but she refused each time with the shake of the head. He wouldn't take no for an answer and eventually Peter stepped off stage and told him to buzz off, that Kelly was with him. He seemed harmless enough and came back later to apologise with a round of drinks for the girls.

Rico and Peter stopped playing at around 11.30pm; they packed their equipment into the van and began larking about on the floor with the girls. As Peter burled Kelly around, she suddenly went limp, doubled over and fell to the floor. The boys both picked her up and sat her down on a chair. At first everyone laughed thinking she'd had too much to drink; Glory B realising that it couldn't have been alcohol for she drank only water, recognised the symptoms immediately 'Good God' she exclaimed as she held Kelly's head firmly to prevent it banging on the table, 'she's been spiked, some one's spiked her water, some bastard's spiked her!'

'You know, I think your right, Glory B' said Rico O Neill in a concerned tone. He knelt down putting his arm around Kelly's shoulders in an attempt to bring her body to an upright position in case she choked. He then suggested getting her into the van and bringing her to the Letterkenny hospitable which was about 40 miles away.

That word, spiked, spread around Nellie's like wildfire and everyone wanted a look, so it was imperative that Kelly was brought to somewhere private and away from prying eyes. Sam Wallace the manager told the boys to take Kelly into his office; he was anxious that the Garda Siochána weren't notified in case it would have an effect on business and his licence renewal application, which was due in August. There had been trouble before in Nellie's with drugs, not from locals but from drug dealers from Belfast and Derry selling drugs to the young people who frequented Nellie's.

Kelly was a dead weight and when the boys tried to stand her up both legs flopped with her knees hitting the floor. Glory B was crying and demanding the Garda be sent for and an ambulance; Kelly couldn't speak but shook her head to indicate she wanted none of it.

'Do you want to go to hospital, Kelly?' Peter spoke slowly and calmly, looking into the hazy eyes of a comatose Kelly; he felt a surge of guilt and a need to get whoever was responsible for this; but first he needed to know that Kelly would be o.k. 'Why would anyone do this, we don't even know anyone here?' Glory B pleaded out loud directing the question to no one in particular and Rico stood close to her like a body guard protecting his charge!

After many cups of black coffee and glasses of water at last Kelly started to come around. She didn't want her dad to know anything about this whole matter; she promised to tell her friend why, later when they were alone. She asked Glory B to ring her mum and say they had gone to a party and not to worry that they would spend the night in

Kelly's hotel room and for Gloria to get Henry to stay the night in her room. Glory B knew that this wasn't going to be an easy sell, given that her mum would twig on that there was more to it; in fact Glory B knew that her mum would think that they were up to no good with the boys. Glory B went out the back to make the call in private; she didn't know how she was going to explain this to her mum without making it sound worse than it was, after all no actual harm had come to Kelly, but at the same time she thought to herself, what if! What if whoever did this had taken Kelly home, it just didn't bear thinking about.

There was no answer to Gloria's mobile so Glory B texted her: ring me urgently and don't tell Henry and I mean urgently xo; looking up as she pressed send Rico appeared in the doorway with just the last thing Glory B wanted to be told. 'I'm afraid you've got company!'

'Tell me you're joking……….' She could see her mum and Henry at the bar laughing with Sam the manager; she rushed to get them away from him or anyone who might tell them what had happened. Glory B nervously laughed as she took her mum by the arm leading them to an empty corner at the far end of the room. 'Well, how did the evening go sweetheart……… where's Kelly?' Before answering, Glory B took a deep breath and felt her face change colour, for lying to her mum was something that was alien to her, honesty and trust were what their relationship was based on and even though this deceit was for Kelly's sake it didn't come easy for Glory B to deceive her mum. It also felt strange that in this crisis she couldn't help but observe Henry's body language towards her mum and her mum's response and that somehow they looked different …………they looked like they were together, really together. Glory B hesitated at first and unlike herself she seemed flustered.

'Well where is Kelly'? Henry asked firmly 'everything all right'?

'Fine, everything's fine, this is Rico, Rico was gigging here tonight, weren't you Rico, this is my mum, Gloria and Kelly's dad, Henry' her voice racing to warn Rico not to blurt out what had happened. She needn't have worried on that score for Rico O Neill could play the devil himself along. 'Kelly's gone on ahead with Rico's fiddler, Peter, we're going to another gig with these handsome and very, very talented musicians, Kelly's doing the tambourine, their tambourine person took sick, too much Guinness I think!'

'Got it in one Glory B' Rico said with unashamed dishonesty!'

Henry didn't know what to think, or believe, he suddenly felt sick as his stomach turned and his mind began racing; she wouldn't, she couldn't, she just...........'Where is this gig........? We'll go too, where is it'? There was a sudden urgency in Henry's tone which Rico picked up on immediately. Rico ask Henry to come outside a moment with him, he wanted to reassure Henry that Kelly was in safe hands with Peter and pointing out that they were both local musicians known by everyone in the area including the bar manager Sam Wallace, who was washing the glasses behind the bar and would vouch that neither of the two had a bad reputation with the girls. He suggested that Henry ask Sam if he was in any doubt. Of course that wasn't strictly true as everyone knew that Rico has a reputation for loving them and leaving them, but in a harmless way; he never went too far in leading a girl on, he usually made his position clear at the start of an encounter that his music would always come first!

Rico's bluff paid off and Henry accepted his word that Kelly was in no danger; though what he was concerned about was if she'd taken anything, drink or drugs; there was no way he was going to ask the question what state Kelly was in for he was certain that if she was in a bad way someone would have come looking for him!

Mother and daughter hugged and kissed after Gloria agreed to coax Henry with all the charm she processed, into staying at Mrs Kelly's for the remainder of the night; Glory B didn't tell her mum the whole story but promised to tell her everything in the morning. Gloria trusted her daughter, she knew that it must be really important for her to be so secretive; she discounted: sex, drugs or drink; she knew her daughter well enough to know it must be something else and probably to do with Kelly, for really, they had only met and knew very little about one another's history. It's situations like this when instinct guides us to do what we believe to be the right thing; for instinct can be a good tool if you don't know the whole story, to trust or not to trust is the question and Gloria had told her daughter often enough to always trust her instincts. Gloria was about to take a leaf out of her own book and do precisely that!

At 2am Henry's mobile rang. It was Kelly 'Sorry dad for messing you about earlier, but I'm having such a great time with Glory B, did her mum tell you she's staying with me tonight?

'Oh baby, you had me worried sick…. everything ok?'

'I knew you'd be worried dad…. Sorry!'

'Be good'

'Love you. Night Night.'

Henry turned to Gloria in Mrs Kelly's lounge, a smile of contentment lit across his face; he winked at her and whispered in her ear 'I think we'll call it a night….now'

He kissed her hand as he helped her up; put his arm around her bare shoulders then floated (as lovers do) toward the stairs!

Chapter 14: The Long Night

The night porter knocked lightly on room 36, bringing a pot of coffee, hot milk and dry toast which the girls had ordered on their way through reception. He was a friendly sort and left the tray on a small table that looked out of place in the 4 star hotel room. 'I'm afraid it's a bit wonky girls!' he remarked, setting the tray down and rocking the table to demonstrate its unevenness. 'Would you like me to pour?' he asked with a touch of class in a rich unidentifiable accent.

'Thank you… kind sir!' Glory B joked. There seemed something familiar about this old porter dressed in a silvery stripped suit that matched his shock of white thick hair parted in the middle and well lacquered to stay behind an enormous pair of pierced ears that were decorated with 4 earrings on each; two sets of silver loops and two white diamond studs. His side-burns met a well-oiled moustache and curiously retained a hint of ginger in them. Glory B was polite with the porter as he introduced himself as Gabriel 'Not Gabriel as in the angel Gabriel, rather, Gabriel as in the Clarence!' He said in a well-rehearsed tone that he used when carrying out his night duties for guests.

'I don't get your accent…..you're not from Donegal!'

'Not originally…………I'm from nowhere in particular' he said looking into Glory B's eyes and freaking her out a little. He was a bit too old to be trying to connect at this hour of the night with a young girl who only wanted a cup of tea from him and nothing else; she didn't go for old swingers and definitely not a Status Quo type groupie that this old porter reminded her off.

'I suppose you get some strange ones staying here at times' it was not so much a question but a remark made in order to be courteous to the old porter as Glory B watched him poured.

'Well now………..' he went to sit down and Glory B immediately began yawning as Kelly walked from the bathroom; aware of the hint he took his leave saying he'd quite a few stories to tell when they had the time. He closed the door softly as he left and swiftly opened it and with his head between the door and frame he quickly said 'before I go….. must tell you the oddest request I ever got through the night, it was for a priest, (an English gent it was) to be brought to this here very room, number 36, it was on a Christmas eve some years back, anyway when the old Father McGinnty arrived, lo and behold, your English man had gone, vanished, didn't even pay his bill!'

The girls stared at the porter blankly in case any sign of interest might encourage him to remove his head from between the door and frame and bring it along with the rest of his silver pin stripped clad body back into the room. His head disappeared and all was quiet in room number 36 for a while.

Wearing Kelly's yellow silk short Victoria's Secret pyjamas, her hair tied back in a ponytail and her long, golden brown legs dangling over the edge of the bed, Glory B looked like a super model posing for a lingerie company. But Kelly looked older now then her 17 years; a harshness masked her lovely face and her eyes looked empty. She wore a short night shirt and Glory B noticed the label was also a Victoria's Secret brand. Kelly's hair was in a mess and Glory B had tried to brush it but couldn't do so without pulling some hair from their roots, so she promised to help straighten it out in the morning. Kelly sat with her head bowed into her knees and suddenly began to sob. Her sobs were painful to hear. Glory B took Kelly's two hands and held them tightly. 'Kelly, what is it that makes you feel so alone?............this isn't just about being spiked, is it? 'Talk, tell me, I'm a good listener, I've got issues, everyone has, but if you need..........if you want to talk........talk to me, it won't leave this room ....promise!.'

Kelly talked and cried, cried and talked, there weren't enough paper hankies so Glory B got a hand towel from the bathroom and Kelly dug her face into it; at first it was as though she was drying her tears but Glory B clicked on that Kelly was hiding her face when she said anything that was painful. Gradually the towel dropped on the floor, and it really developed into a one to one. Both had open wounds from the past, wounds that neither parent knew were wounds; but each couldn't just tell the other their story like it was a bedtime story where afterward the book is closed and everyone lives happily ever after. These wounds still stung when the air got to them; granted they weren't aired unless someone left the metaphorical door open to let all the puss spill out! At around 6am it felt good to have had someone to talk to, someone to listen, someone to share with; and side by side they both fell into a beautiful sleep. True friendship was born in room number 36 Madden's B&B this very night between two girls who were no longer strangers.

The fan didn't hum as much when the speed was turned down from 3 to 2 and finally to number 1; in the quiet of the night it was initially a distraction for Henry who was used to a noiseless environment in his own bedroom back in Boston; but now the irritation of the fan faded into oblivion as he and Gloria, lying side by side in the cosy iron bed in room number 33 enjoyed the physical closeness to another body and the emotional sparks that were waiting to be ignited at any moment; could this be really happening to them, it was like a dream come true, come from nowhere, they were connected, like a plug and a socket, the electricity running through them, it was a question of que sera, sera.

It wasn't easy to get Henry to lie alongside of her but she teased him saying she wouldn't attack unless provoked! Neither wanted to rush things nor to make this into a one-night-stand. They both knew that something special was happening between them. Gloria blotted the tumour and the thought of going home completely out of her head. This experience with Henry Dickson bordered on spiritual; it felt……..beautiful; Gloria could think of no words in the English language to describe the way she was feeling; but she was prompted by a saying in Irish that her father used to say, it felt a bit strange just to remember it out of the blue like this. 'Anam Cara' she whispered to Henry, their lips almost meeting.

'Anam Cara to you………' she opened her mouth to catch his warm breath before explaining its meaning.

'Soul friend...........but I think we're going to be much more....'

'What can be more than friends of the soul?........ What can be deeper than the sea'? he sighed.

'I can do better than that' she jested, 'let's see, to follow that last philosophical tease, deeper than the sea, right, right, here goes......now don't try to put me of..... right here goes again...........in my bed of sea..........will you swim or drown with me!' They both laughed and looking into one another's eyes for what seemed like forever. Henry broke the mystical silence, 'we're not going to drown..........the way I feel about you........Gloria, I'm a man who could walk on water' She closed her eyes and he moved over her body and they kissed. Then the familiar ring of Gloria's mobile ruined the moment; both thought that something had happened to the girls and they jumped up in a panic trying to find where the mobile was; by the time they found it, it had stopped ringing. Gloria didn't recognise the number so she rang back, her heart thumping and Henry almost expecting the call to be about Kelly.

'Hello, who is this, you've just rang me, who are you?'

The voice at the other end was Julie's. 'Are you in Mrs Kelly's you'll never believe what's.........' and the phone went dead. Henry fell down on the edge of the bed, relieved. Gloria stood frozen on the spot still holding the mobile and trying to ring back but the recorded voice of someone called Sammy came on informing callers that he was busy at the moment and if they left a message he would get back to them as soon as possible.

'I'm stunned…………… stunned, Julie obviously doesn't know about the time difference between here and Nashville or where ever she is! I bet it's big trouble, she must be in jail or something, trust Julie' as she threw the mobile across the room hitting the soft chair by the dressing table she cursed, which was something she seldom did. Julie, wait till I get you, spoil sport, she thought to herself. Maybe Julie's timing wasn't all that wrong, maybe it was spot on before they got too carried away, Gloria laughed out loud and jumped back into bed. 'It's cold now, come on warm me up, hold me, come on, we can talk'. She pulled back the bedclothes letting Henry in beside her.

'If you prefer to wait………I can wait' he said it like a man who was in control, a strong honest man; and he touched her face gently and winked sending Gloria's emotions to paradise. Oh God, she thought, what am I doing with this gorgeous man in my bed! She couldn't recall anyone else she'd gone out with being so handsome, things were looking up; but then she remembered……………

'I can wait…….hold me and talk to me' she whispered. But inside she wished they hadn't been interrupted and now she feared that the tumour would cut down the middle of the bed, like a blade to separate Gloria and her new found love! Suddenly the word, tumour, filled her mind and she felt lost, alone, destitute, where could she go, what was going to happen her when she got back to Belfast! A moment ago she felt so happy, why had this happened, what had she ever done that was so wrong that she should be cursed by this. Henry noticed Gloria seemed far away, Then as he stroked her forehead she recognised an irony as he said 'what I'd give to be inside that lovely head of yours……….tell me, what goes on inside there?'

A light mist had descended over Fundoran and the smell of turf burning crept into every room at Mrs Kelly's; even though there were no open windows in room 33 the smell woke Henry up; he gently moved Gloria's head from his chest where she had enjoyed listening to him tell her things he wanted her to know about his life. The rich smell reminded Henry of his childhood in Boston. His father, who was always first up in the mornings would have the coffee pot on the range; he smiled to himself remembering that the aroma was like the family alarm clock, when you smelt it you knew it was time to get up and get ready.   Henry felt warm inside as he looked at this beautiful woman asleep beside him. He felt good that he and Gloria were two of a kind, Anam Cara's, as Gloria had put it.

As he stood on the veranda clad in blue boxers watching scores of birds playing along the sea front, a young boy with short red curly hair, wearing long pink silky pyjama bottoms on a white horse came galloping along the wet sand being chased and then overtaken by countless sea gulls, the majestic creature followed them to where the sand met the rocks then turned to retrace it's footsteps back along the outgoing tide. It was 5.30am and Henry breathed deeply to fill his lungs with the fresh sea air. He stood looking out across the sea thinking that he could belong here, it would be so easy to want to stay…………. with Gloria by his side. He gave his heart so easily but this time he felt it was right, somehow he knew that Gloria felt the same! Watching the horse and boy disappear in the distance his thoughts turned to his daughter and he wondered how she had been and he said a prayer that everything had gone well for her last night and that she was in a safe and happy place in her mind and also in a peaceful sleep. A shiver ran through him as he reluctantly remembered when things were bad at home with Kelly, that every night he would pray that she would fall into a peaceful sleep before her friends would call on the cell phone wanting her to go out with them. Her going out at night was his nightmare. But things felt so good now between them that Henry wanted so much to believed that that was all behind them and the past was now past and gone forever; but still, a tiny doubt still haunted him with painful memories from then; he would just have to trust Kelly and this was what giving her space last night was all about.

Gloria sneezed then stretched her long thin arms under the pillow and without opening her blue and brown eyes, she took a deep breathe inhaling every ounce of Henry's scent that now clung to ruffled linen sheets and she flung the pillow landing it at his feet. Picking it up he gently threw it back and taking a leap landed almost on top of her. They laughed and Gloria giggled like a child who hadn't yet lost her innocence while enjoying being tickled under her arms and on the soles of her feet, sending the most sensual electric shocks through all her body; she gasped loudly at the sheer pleasures her unaccustomed body was being treated to. The bed was a complete mess as they rolled over and up and down on top of one another laughing, surprising, tickling and then finally, gazing into one another's eyes, they kissed passionately; this time there would be no stopping, no being sensible, no waiting, this was here and now and they knew the moment had finally arrived when each would forsake all the self-promises to tread carefully and go slowly and not rush things like a couple of teenagers. Nothing to do with being sensible mattered at this moment the ship that was carrying them was going full steam ahead.

Suddenly there was banging at the door and a familiar voice in low sharp shouts called out.

Henry was easing his body down on Gloria's when they both froze and Henry fell limp to her side.

'What the hell'

'It can't be………..Julie…… is that you? How the hell!'

'Open up, just open up!'

Henry pulled his boxers up and jumped to open the door.

Julie fell in. She was wearing a white nylon scarf over her head and tied at the back of her neck, large white rimmed sunglasses and a very distinct Chanel white and navy spotted trouser suit with matching extra-large handbag. Without looking at Henry she ran throwing herself face down on the bed, started crying (fake of course), Julie was so dramatic, a typical diva, and the two lovers just stared wondering if this was really happening.

'Julie………what are you doing here………you went to Nashville……..what's happened……..bye the way, this is Henry'.

Julie eased herself up on her elbows and smiled at Henry who was putting his trousers on 'please don't on my account!'

'Julie,' Gloria kept repeating over and over until Henry decided he would leave them and get an early breakfast if he could find anywhere opened at this hour; if not a walk along the beach would do nicely. As he closed the door he turned and winked at Gloria, she blew him a kiss and lipped 'later.'

'Looks like I disturbed something…………gee Gloria, you'll never guess what happened, I'm not sure if I believe it myself…………..' Gloria looked in amazement at her friend and said as though checking her own sanity 'Julie, you did go to Nashville…….didn't you?

'Yeah, I did go and I even went to see Chrystal Gale and she sang Don't it make my brown eyes blue and I thought of you and what you were missing; she was even better than I'd ever imagined and that was how I met him.' Julie had this habit of when she was telling you something and you didn't make a noise to indicate every so often that you were still listening (such as an: ah, or oh or umm) she'd say 'are you listening?' with a strong emphases on the you. But now this was the cookie of them all and Gloria sat amazed with mouth wide opened waiting to hear some fantastic tale of situation comedy, that over the years of their friendship she had become accustomed too. It usually took Julie a while to get to the point but now she delivered the punch line at the beginning of her story.

'You're what!' Gloria laughed out loud.

'It's not funny……..I'm afraid and in big trouble'

'What are you on?'

'Right this is it, this is all I know……….I woke up three days ago in a motel, a seedy motel at that, the bathroom was filthy……..in Las Vegas…….I didn't know at the time it was Las Vegas………and there he was next to me in bed……….still wearing his Elvis tee shirt, I eased myself my fully clothed self out of bed, he turned over still snoring, and I couldn't believe it………..it was……….. surreal, I felt like I was standing in The Bates Motel from Psycho and that at any second he'd jump up with a knife in his hand and plunge it into me; it was so so unreal; I don't think I've ever been so afraid in my entire life before;

excluding of course that time in the Dunville Park when that big Alsatian belonging to Joe Black chased and bit me on the leg, remember, I ended up with nine stitches. Are you listening?' Putting her hand on Gloria's leg and shaking it to make sure she was paying proper attention to the story. Gloria stared and nodded like someone who was being hypnotised.

'Had to go for a wee, didn't flush, spotted my passport and his, tip toed round to his side of the bed, I couldn't read his name, I think it was Russian, and then……….. in black and white, a marriage certificate with my name on it……… we were married, yes married; the proof was there in my trembling hand. I can't even pronounce his name, it began with a Y…….I think his surname began with a P, Puddin or something like that……….why oh why do things like this always happen to me……….' three times Julie's mouth opened but nothing came out, it seemed to Gloria that her mind wasn't properly connected at this moment to her mouth; then at last she said with a tremor in her upper lip, 'that's all I can remember about it! When, I got to the door, didn't look back, just ran and ran and ran. It was like a dream, there was a bus with the engine running and I made it as the doors were about to close; it was like a chariot just waiting there for me, to rescue me, take me away. The driver Charlie kept me right.'

Gloria smiled at that because with Julie there was always a man around every corner.

'I got another bus to somewhere and then to Newark airport and………here I am. It took hours, I watched day turn into night and back to day and yet I've no idea how I got there in the first place!'

'Where's the certificate?'

'I ate it……..what else could I do!'

'Julie, Julie, Julie' holding her hands tightly and searching her mischievous face for an ounce of sense, she said in a serious tone 'you know now, officially, you're what's known as a bigamist!'

'Who's to know'……….she said with a hint of a cry in her voice 'being married to an extra-terrestrial doesn't count; E.T didn't perform in the wedding bed……he took one of his panic attacks or so he led me to believe, but how naive was I then, I'd have believed anything he told me; all I was left with was his fake empty wallet; everything in my life turns out to be fake, she spoke with an energy in her tone of someone who was not put down by things that did not always go to plan for her. I'm going off on one here, you know Gloria, I never told you this bit before but he even lied that he'd bought return tickets back to Belfast, I hadn't two pence to rub together; he'd taken all my savings for safe keeping well, that's how he put it and I'd to get home before anyone missed me. I never told the family about the marriage or Eric they still don't know to this day that I got married; that I'd become Mrs Eric Trotter. Oh God, what am I like? He may as well have vanished back to outer space the next morning when he said he was going out to the shop to get me a bar of chocolate. I was easy pleased in those days! I don't think I'll ever see him again…….teenage sweethearts ran all the way to Gretna Green and for what? For him to see if he could do it! I wonder if he's still alive, maybe the heat killed him out in where ever you go with the French Legion. I don't care and this is just another one of those experiences, but this time I just haven't a clue, I don't remember, I think he must have drugged me or something!'

'But how would he have got you from Nashville to Vegas without you waking up, it's not just down the road Julie!'

'Well, I remember - I think, bits and pieces, I remember laughing a lot and……….boozing, the booze was………oh God, I feel sick thinking about it; but, Gloria, it's done, what's done is done, that's my motto, you know that……and if he can't trace me then I'll get it out of my mind somehow! Say I hadn't seen the marriage cert, then I wouldn't have known that I got married at all……..this is all crazy, even getting back here it's all a bit fuzzy but

I'm certain we didn't do anything', Unseen by Gloria, Julie crossed her fingers behind her back. 'I feel the same as I always feel, if you know what I mean!'

They would have to talk later, but for now Julie needed to sleep so Gloria tucked her up in bed and lay beside her, stroking her hair back from her head until she fell into a deep sleep.

In a darker moment as Gloria watched her friend sleep peacefully, sadness filled her heart and tears began to flow silently; she wondered what would become of Julie if she wasn't around to pick up the pieces! Despite the funny faces Julie always wore there was the vulnerable, easily hurt Julie that Gloria knew so well and she shivered as the sky outside darkened as though it were preparing for thunder. Gloria closed the veranda doors and Ali's words stormed her mind: Don't count the days…. make the days count.'

The thunder roared and the rain poured down and Gloria was happy that Julie was here, safe, asleep and with someone who really cared about her.

Chapter 15: Kissing Cousins?

The two girls slept soundly, oblivious to the thunder and pouring rain that brought life back into the crusted earth. It was around 10.30am when Henry carried a tray of coffee, tea and toast into the room. He entered cautiously then breathed a sigh of relief to find them actually there. He smiled as he thought to himself old habits die hard. From past experience Henry knew the best course of action when entering Kelly's room the morning after the night before was: to tread carefully, say nothing, show no sign of surprise or anger and to expect the unexpected which sometimes to his relief would have been nothing at all. He switched the radio on to gently wake them and to his surprise and delight one of his favourite songs was playing; A Little Time by The Beautiful South; Henry couldn't help but sing along: a little bit of time to think it over, a little bit of space to think it out, need a little room to………. Kelly woke first and Henry kissed her on the cheek, 'did you have a good night sweetheart?'

'I love you dad' she said softly as she stretched her arms; Glory B pretended to be still asleep; just for that moment she wished she had a father to bring her breakfast; not so much for the breakfast itself but the gesture behind it.

'I've news for Glory B when she wakes!'

'Hope it's not that you've got my mum pregnant!' a little voice came from half under the sheet.

'Shame on you for thinking that your mum and I would………..'

Kelly quickly interacted 'Can we please change the subject………..it's too early in the morning to have this type of conversation!…………look at this daddy, I've chipped a nail' they all laughed and Kelly held her hand out for Henry to kiss it better. When Henry told Glory B that Julie had arrived and was with her mum down at Mrs Kelly's, she shrugged her shoulders and wondered what the story would be this time. Glory B liked Julie and appreciated the fact that her mum shared that sort of carefree happy-go-lucky type relationship with Julie; but there was something about Julie that attracted people (in general) but (men in particular) who always seemed to turn the most ordinary situations into circus rings. Julie always seemed to lose her man; she never held onto a man for long and Glory B didn't quite know if it was a Julie thing or the man thing!

'Haven't ever driven one of these before, in fact, never seen a real one' said Henry to the garage man.

'You're from the USA mister, wasn't sure, thought maybe you were Canadian!................don't know what you yanks were missing then back in the 70's and 80's,' replied the garage man in a slow droll. 'Tell you what, take her for the day, fill her up and I'll not charge you a cent mister........ as long as you get her back here for 6 o clock!'

'What if I'm a few minutes late?'

'You pay me for a week's rental in that case!'

'O.K. then, suits me' as Henry turned, the garage man gave Gloria the eye behind his back; she smiled inwardly at the idea of it; Fundoran was always a great place for clicking! 'What about you girls, 6 o clock suit you?' the three girls all agreed. 'Back for 6 it is then!' Henry went into the garage man's office to get the keys and on the way out he tripped over an open paint tin and almost fell flat on his face, saved by his hands but left with paint sticking to his shoes. The garage man told Henry he couldn't drive his car, his rented car, with paint on his soles, but lucky for Henry they both took a size 10 and Mr Fixit, as Gloria called him under her breath, had indeed a spare pair of mosses sandals he kept for emergencies (the mind boggles). So finally they drove off, with Mr Fixit shouting after Henry to keep to the left side of the road!

'What is this car anyway?' asked Kelly.

'It's a Lada……………..Russian make.

'Not even a nice colour!' remarked Gloria 'drab….ish even!'

'Quaint………ish…where did he find it! Bet it was bartered!'

'What with?...........a horse drawn carriage!' replied Glory B; the mood was jovial and witty in that clapped up Lada as it steered its way down the country roads towards Ballyshannon in search of knowledge from a time that was once lived by the O Neill clan and to River Cottage their once upon a time home where secrets from the past might shock Henry and enlighten Kelly to who she really is!

Sure enough there was a river gently flowing through the garden of River Cottage and two elderly women dressed in matching pinafores waiting outside the half front door each supporting themselves on identical walking sticks, one with her right hand and the other with the left; Henry noticed this because both he and Kelly were left handed and so also had his father been left handed.

'Oh God, is this real,' Kelly said as the car pulled up making choking noises as smoke bellowed from the engine. Henry turned and looking into Kelly's eyes said 'Here at last…………..as promised' he smiled and thought to himself, déjà vu; both stepping from the Lada into the warm embrace from the sisters, the smell of turf and the familiarity of the primrose painted cottage gave the pilgrims an immediate sense of belonging.

'Tá me ag Moira'

'agus tá me ag Roslin………..cead me ag failthe to River Cottage, Henry agus Kelly, one hundred thousand welcomes to our great nephew Henry O'Neill- Dickson and your beautiful daughter! Welcome!

'I see you're like me, a cloot!' he addressed Roslin.

'Ciotógach' like your father……….'

'And Kelly's left handed as well'………that seemed to please Roslin; she took Kelly's hand and headed into the cottage.

'Is this more family' asked Moira referring to Gloria and Glory B.

'Friends, good friends, Moira!'

'I recognise that twinkle in your eye, it's an O'Neill trait, and it says so much without uttering a word, you're

Johnboy's son indeed; now bring them in, don't leave them out there, the kettle's on and there are freshly baked scones, enough for all our guests! ' She spoke in a soft almost whispered tone and there was a melody as the words flowed unmeasured from her painted tight red lips. Henry hadn't known what to expect so he was happy that the sisters seemed kindly people. There was so much Henry wanted to find out, so much he needed to know about all his relations and although he'd only met his great aunts moments ago he could feel somehow that he was like them, like the O'Neill's and that made him feel good about who he was.

The sisters told him how much they had loved his father Johnboy and how grieved they were about his untimely death and then Henry's mother never corresponded with them afterwards so they were hurt and mystified as to why; but years later they'd heard that she'd remarried within the year of Johnboy's dying! Henry explained; his mother could neither read nor write and she was so lost and vulnerable after his father died that she picked up with a neighbours lodger, Tom Dickson. It was never a happy union but it was bearable for Henry although he was for most of the time ignored. Tom was a possessive man and one of the things he made his mother do was to change Henry's name from O'Neill to Dickson. They moved house after the marriage so Henry moved school as well and so then everyone would know him as Dickson. It was like my dad was wiped from my memory; I wasn't allowed to mention his name, but I kept alive the years I spent with him, I never once forgot his birthday........ Roslin cut in 'February 5th...........no one in Ballyshannon forgot him either!' There were a few more sad moments that changed when they went indoors.

Inside River Cottage was as much fairy tale like as the outside was with its thatched roof, pale pink rambling roses that stretched across each window top over to the open half front door where they cascaded like tiny ringlets from a child's head. There were four chumps of long grasses with furry tips that small birds could use as a swing to break the monotony of hot summer days and lupines and gladiolas standing guard in their colourful magnificence against a decaying walled entrance to a separate section of garden; of course the jewel in the centre of this idyllic paradise was the river; imagine having a river on your doorstep Henry mused to himself. As each entered the cottage they gasped in amazement at the sheer eloquence, brightness and sparkle that took them by surprise. The French doors to the back of the living room were open;

the rich fragrance from the purple haze of lavender that lined a cobbled pathway was everywhere adding to the tranquilly contagious mood of this timeless room.

Homemade raspberry jam melted on the hot scones: china cups and saucers, silver tiny tea spoons, linen embroidered table cloth, a glass cabinet with 3 shelves all holding dolls: china dolls, rag dolls and a large doll wearing a discoloured white lace brides dress with vale; its chin pieced noticeably back together (they would be told the story later of how the doll was broken) From the ceiling above the French doors hung a thread with 3 crystal stones, their coloured sparkle touched every wall in the room and turned the grey stone floor into the end of a rainbow; a pot of gold sitting on the floor would not have looked out of place in such an enchanting room. Perfection……… Gloria thought, everything was perfect; it was like being read a fairy-tale at bedtime and actually wanting to sleep to become part of it all; but Gloria was awake there was no need to sleep to make it feel real; it was real, for now at least!

Moving out to the back garden to talk more and enjoy listening about all the O'Neill family and some astonishing family secrets that with all the years that have passed since their happening now only seemed like trivialities; although in their time it was all so shameful and embarrassing for the O'Neill clan. For example: kissing cousins. It embarrassed Henry to be told that several of his great aunts and uncles had had romantic inclinations towards one another, and that those who had succumbed to pressure from the hierarchy of the clan into marrying someone they didn't love for respectability sake, well their marriages were all doomed to failure…….. without exception; though none ever separated but nonetheless there must have been a lot of terribly unhappy O'Neill's running about in Ballyshannon during the last century. 'You must understand, Henry' said Roslin, 'the O'Neill clan was massive, we were everywhere; in our family there were sixteen of us, eight boys and eight girls, and in uncle Patsy's family there were eighteen, uncle James family was the smallest with only seven. You could go nowhere here without meeting an O Neill.' Henry wasn't sure that he wanted to know the whole story of the O Neill clan now, but for Kelly's sake he put the question to the sisters; 'what about addictions and tumours, anything in that line? The sisters were amused at Henry's choice of questions and his directness; surely he hadn't sought them out, all the way from America to ask only those two questions, but then they weren't to know his reasoning behind it.

There had been no criminals in the clan, though many had suffered prison at the hands of the British but for honourable reasons, and no, came the reply, there was never any addictions as far as they both knew, but sadly haemorrhages and tumours of different kinds did seem to have been the cause of many a sudden O Neill death. Gloria and Glory B shared a glance at this piece of information and Gloria thought to herself that now she just could not share with Henry her recently diagnosed tumour, she would kiss and say good bye in a few days' time, and that would be that! He could resume his life in Boston as before, and she, Gloria from Belfast, would definitely not go gently into the night; Henry would not be part of the ending to her story, for now, she was determined he must never know! The word tumour would definitely scare him off and she preferred to keep her dreams and good thoughts about their meeting intact, in case she should need them for any lonely nights.

The roar of an engine being pulled to a sudden halt disturbed the peacefulness of the garden 'that must be Richard' the two sisters smiled sweetly awaiting their great nephew to make his entrance.

'He promised to come to meet you, he's a musician………. did we say that music runs through the veins of all us O'Neill's' Moira laughed, 'the most important thing about us and we almost forgot to mention it'

Everyone turned as the click of studded boots got closer and to their amazement in marched……….Rico.

'You son of a bitch' Kelly murmured to herself.

Henry jumped up and shook hands with Rico; everyone was amazed to discover that they'd already met and knew Rico from the previous night.

'Did you know who we were?…………this is just fantastic………….more than coincidence don't you think?' He waited for Rico's reply.

'I sort of guessed yesterday…………'

'Why didn't you say?'

Laughter broke out and more scones were put on the table and everyone was happy, well almost everyone.

Photographs and stories were exchanged and a real sense of family enveloped the setting; Peter arrived; himself, Rico, Kelly and Glory B decided to do a tour of Ballyshannon; Rico wanted the girls to see The Rory

Gallaher Exhibition; he was an expert as was Peter on every aspect of Rory's life. Rory Gallaher was one of their icons whom in their early musical endeavours they had tried to emulate him; everyone wanted to be like Rory and now his untimely death did not diminish that desire in young musicians to aspire to that same individuality and greatness as this Ballyshannon son had achieved.

Good-byes and kisses were exchanged and promises to call the following day were confirmed by Kelly as the sisters stood with Henry and Gloria to wave the foursome off and in character Rico had to have the last word as they drove off in a puff of choking smoke, he shouted waving his left hand through the open window 'yee haa………. up all lefties' and then rhymed lyrically '……..up the airy mountain…. down the rushy glen….we daren't go a-hunting………for fear of little men…………..wee folk…good folk…..trooping all together……green………' and with the smokey bang bang from the exhaust pipe they were gone. Henry stayed a while longer and was amazed to discover that the sisters were on email, they even had their own web-site; THE BALLYSHANNON BRANCH OF THE O'NEILL CLAN It was amazing to think that at their age they were into surfing the net and Henry said so only to be told not to patronise, as it was unbecoming of an O'Neill!

It had been a wonderful day for Henry and now he and Gloria were heading back to Fundoran early to make sure that he didn't have to pay for the car; and also Gloria was anxious to be there for Julie when she woke up. But fate and the Lada joined forces to play a hand in costing Henry the price of the week's hire of the conspiratorial Russian made car! But soon Henry would realise that what lay ahead could neither be bought nor paid for with money; for things of the heart are priceless. Somewhere along the way they took a left turn instead of a right and the road led them to a small fishing place called Burtonport. It was miles away from Fundoran and they seemed to have been driving for ages. They passed a hotel called The Viking House and a young fellow who looked strikingly like Daniel O Donnell himself holding a large tea pot was there and a crowd of around a few hundred people mostly women all standing around drinking cups of tea; they stopped and Gloria took directions from a woman standing on the road side drinking her tea; 'straight down the road till you see a crossroads and take the left which will lead you into Dungloe, and you're on the right road to Letterkenny, if you take the right instead of the left, then that brings you into Burtonport itself, you can get the ferry there and that'll take you to Aranmore' said the woman taking another sip of her tea.

'We aren't looking to go to Aranmore or Letterkenny!..........it's Fundoran we want'

'hawl on a minute till I get Bridget, she'll be able to put you right……..Bridget' she called out and impulsively Henry put his foot on the accelerator and belted down the road doing about 15mph. The screams and yahoo's from inside the car made Henry lose control for an instant as he swerved to avoid a lone sheep that seemed to come from out of nowhere; the tea drinking crowd may have mistaken himself and Gloria for a couple of joy-riders; though, that's unlikely!

On they went and to the right Gloria spotted a beach sign that was actually nailed onto a tree. Not just any ordinary beach sign, but this one stated a secluded beach. 'Have you ever been to a secluded beach…… before'?

'Before what?' Henry gamely replied. And the atmospherics in the clapped up Lada were lustful. Every movement every gesture every murmur and sigh was dripped in desire and need! But would there be any satisfaction at the end of this particular road?

They turned off the main road and followed the beach sign or rather their instincts. The road wasn't really a road but more of a dirt track but the little cottages and lakes strewn over the rocky hills were breath-taking. Finally they came to where they could go no further. The Lada was halted and they both stared at the sight in front of them. The Atlantic Ocean was so calm and blue and across was a little island that was in paddling distance. The car was perched almost on the edge of a bank that wasn't visible from inside the car, but when they got out they realised how high up they were. There was no sign of the temperature dropping, the early morning thunder and rain was a prelude to more sweltering heat. Hand and hand they walked across the top of the grassy bank, their feel feeling the softness of the underlying sand that had been gathering for thousands of years; they slowly made their way down to another beach and presumably this was the secluded beach mentioned on the sign post. They took their sandals off but quickly put them on again; the sand was burning their soles; but there was a greater fire burning inside them, a fire that was not to be extinguished with such a simple remedy.

There were no foot prints in the sand and no other sign of anyone being around which prompted Gloria to say suggestively 'this is virgin territory, we're walking where no one else has walked today' to which Henry replied

'How far do you reckon we will have to go before we find that it's not entirely……..virgin territory?'

'as far as we have too……….I suppose!' they stopped and kissed, gently at first and then their passion uncontrollable with the sureness that they were completely alone brought them to their knees on the scorching sand. They both yelled in instant pain with shock of the burning sand and quickly getting up they moved in unison hand in hand, with passion pulping within them to the shelter of towering rocks. Once they reached the rocks they discovered that there were two massive rocks that were connected by a carpeted grass lawn; how the grass was so short and smooth was a mystery to Henry but Gloria knew that there must be sheep or goats about somewhere. The crevices in the rocks were massive and the white foam came splashing in and out between the rocks on every third wave.

Henry, who was not known for impulsive behaviour, for the second time today, was about to do something that even he knew was uncharacteristic of Henry Dickson; though maybe not so uncharacteristic of a younger Henry

O' Neill.

'Have you ever gone skinny dipping……….?'

'no'

'neither have I………….let's do it………..together' they smiled and began to take their clothes off. Holding hands they faced one another naked……..not looking at the others body, just searching for that something in the eyes, something deep and meaningful, a recognition perhaps of absolute honesty and surrender and equilibrium; each taking a deep sigh they ran to the edge of the bank and together jumped. Hitting the warm water that swallowed them and in their nakedness their bodies melted into one mould of perfect symmetry. Resurfacing was like being reborn; born into a paradise, freed from all physical restrictions; if they were birds this would have been the moment when the egg cracked open and they were born into a new world of wonder. The returning waves pulled them out to the opening of the corridor where the sea entered the gap between the rocks and then the third oncoming wave pushed them back; the mouth of the corridor was narrow so the force of the waves would break down entering the narrow gap between the rocks. The feeling was like nothing on earth. The waves were gentle on their skin, it was like being touched all over in every crevice, every inch of skin soothed by an expert masseur, so expert that they were touched everywhere at once and the effect was calm and peace; they felt so completely at one with the universe. They floated in a state of utopia and when their bodies came together again, it was like heaven. The pureness of the foam added to their inner sense of completeness as they handed themselves over to the power or force, which ever it was, that engulfed them in this new world experience.

Getting out of the water was like a baby being waned from its mother's breast! It was with reluctance they left the sphere of this watered world that had so unexpectedly given them the joy and freedom to share with each other, each other! Once you have suckled it stays with you for ever. A joy beyond compare came over them both as they lay naked on the soft grass; with eyes wide open they touched and felt what at that moment they knew had never been touched in them before……..ever……. and they were both consumed by a passion that under the cloudless sky soared within them to a place neither had ever been…………nor even knew existed.

Chapter 16:
When Love Becomes Clear

Not a single word was spoken on the journey back to Fundoran. There was no need. Words could not convey nor add in any way to the elation that Henry and Gloria had experienced. Gloria, for most of the journey sat as close to Henry as was possible; when she wasn't admiring his face and hands and strong arms she was gently touching his face, running her fingers through his hair, kissing his arm and neck and feeling the lobe of his ear between her fingertips. It was getting dark and they stopped three times in all to give way to passion. Was this love? It was the most wonderful love that Gloria had ever experienced and Henry was certain it was real and intense and true love. It was so long since he felt this good. He had loved Teresa with all his heart and soul; he knew now that he was in love with Gloria.

Everyone was worried about them. The Lada after all was quite old and its road worthiness was questionable. Julie was on the scene, she was up and ready for a night out; she had been told by Glory B who was delighted to see her, about the state and age of the car so Julie went to see the garage man and convinced him to ring the Garda in case they'd had an accident. Julie, in her usual chatty way got the whole run down on the garage man. His name was Ray and he was a widower approaching sixty with no children. He took a fancy to Julie and thought her concern for Gloria was her way of chatting him up; but she was finished with men altogether, for now at least.

The garage man, Julie, the two girls and also Rico and Peter sat on the bench outside the garage awaiting the return of Henry, Gloria and the Lada. A broad smile broke across Ray's face as he recognised instantly the choke, choke of the Lada struggling but determined as it turned the bend a few hundred yards up the road. There was a roar and lots of cheers when the engine conked out just in front of the petrol pumps. 'She knows she's home' murmured Ray as if the Lada was a child of his! Everyone kissed and by way of explanation Henry said that the car had broken down and then they got lost; but Julie could not be fooled she could see there was something different about her best friend, no one knew Gloria like Julie knew her!

Julie linked arms with Gloria and ushered her from the welcoming party but also knowingly from the gaze of Henry. He tried to pursue the linked couple but Julie was too wise for the competition and turning to Henry said jokingly 'you've had her all day, now, it's my turn' she turned on her heels and defiantly moved on towards Mrs Kelly's where they could catch up on their latest exchange stories without being disturbed; but really, Gloria's world was disturbed by Henry, he had turned it upside down and it was wonderful; she wanted Henry to spend the night with her in the privacy of her room and in the softness of the bed that awaited them! She understood Julie's need to talk about Nashville and Las Vegas and what she could remember of it and off course her new husband! But, at this moment Gloria was falling deeper and deeper in love and needed more than anything to be with her lover. Her ration of passion this time around had come in abundance and it was great!

The young set were off to The Green Hut, a small intimate place with a put up bar. Rico and Peter were doing this gig for charity; Fr Hanna was taking the money at the door and was pleased with the donations which he would send off to 'Street Kids Project', a charity ran by a Belfast couple Anne and Paul who were working with street children out in Brazil and Kelly was surprised to learn that Rico was intending to volunteer to go there shortly and help with a building project that the money made tonight was going towards; her perception of him was about to change dramatically!

Kelly wore her hair in an up-style and it made her look older than her 17 years. Both girls enjoyed the crack with Fr Hanna who was quite handsome and clad in faded blue jeans and white open necked grandfather shirt. They were surprised to learn that Rico had been in a seminary for two years and that he'd only left six months ago. 'Why did he leave? Kelly asked curiously.

'You'll have to ask Rico that…………..priesthood doesn't suit everyone who wants to be a priest. Young men nowadays have their own notion of how they want to serve God in what some of them call, the real world, but it doesn't get much realer than the world where this money's destined for!'

'Yeah' said Glory B 'but you don't have to be a priest to help people'

'Of course not, each to their own' and at that the break was announced and Fr Hanna mounted the make-shift stage of several empty beer crates with a few strips of solid wood on top and a black curtain fixed neatly round the edges hiding the unsightly crates; unfortunately the crates moved as the boys jumped off and Fr Hanna stepped on, collapsing the whole set to an instant standing ovation from the amused crowd; there were plenty of helpers to put it right in a short time. As this was happening Rico and Kelly's eyes met and there was a feeling running through their bodies that neither could have foresaw; it was for them that indubitable fatal attraction………….!

No one had missed them; Kelly stood up and fixed her mini skirt down properly and made sure none of the hard strands of hay were stuck to her back as Rico pulled her close to his bare chest then stumbled a little pulling his trousers up with his y fronts sticking in the zip.

'Can I help' she asked.

'You already have' he answered fumbling with the zip in the dark.

'Look, I'm a bit of an expert in this field' she said softly; 'pardon the pun' and lifting her long, smooth, tanned leg, she placed her sandal on the wrong foot.

He managed to get his zip up and took two steps backwards to look at Kelly's face in the moonlight. She looked even more beautiful than anyone he'd ever seen in his life, he thought. She stood tall and slender and with some of her up style now slipping down on her bare shoulders; he thought she looked somewhat vulnerable; but she really wasn't vulnerable, she knew exactly what she wanted and how to get it and at this moment it was Rico………her cousin!

'How do you feel………..now?'

'Crazy………just crazy…………..I guess!'

'You are crazy……………this is just crazy……..I mean, we're blood!'

'Yeah, but not close blood, if you want to analyse it, we've only met, we don't even know anything about each other! All I know is that I hated you and now…….we've done something……… wonderful………we've shared love….. we've made love………love! Not sex………..I know sex and that wasn't it…..that was something else and anyway we're what………three, four times removed………..that's not close blood…….come off it!'

He moved across to where she stood and put his finger across her lips to seal them and stop her saying another word. She kissed and sucked his finger into her mouth and then they kissed passionately each longing to lie down together again; but they were disturbed by distant voices coming in their direction, maybe lovers, like them who needed to share and spend their passion as one; but how could anyone else be like them for when all was said and done, they were still from the same blood; though several times removed, it niggled at the back of Kelly's mind if that would be how Henry would see it. He need never know, Kelly thought; and that seemed naturally logical to her!

Back in The Green Hut, Gloria B and Peter were in deep conversation; they too had discovered that they had much in common and neither seemed to mind later when it became obvious that there was something going on between Rico and Kelly. 'This is a night for gazing up at the stars and watching as the moon disappears into the morning light' Rico announced rather poetically and surprisingly to the whole company which included Father Hanna.

'Explain yourself, young man!' said Father Hanna sportingly.

'Well, who's game for going up to the river, lighting a fire and drowning ourselves in music, song and laughter and being witnesses to the breaking of a new dawn…. well – any takers?'

They all laughed and raised their glasses repeating after Rico 'witnesses to a new dawn'. There was something so intriguing so wanting about this plan and both girls thought in their own different way oh boy how can we refuse that!

When the text messages bleeped it gave both parents the excuse they needed to contact one another. Gloria had been only half listening to Julie for the past two hours and now she would have to rush out to see how Henry felt about the girls staying out in the open un-chaperoned overnight. It wasn't an issue at all, more an opportunity for them to be together; was fate being generous to them tonight?

After lying to Julie that she'd be back in 10 minutes she rushed into Henry's arms and then ……his bed! No one had ever made love to Gloria like this; it was the stuff that every woman's fantasy was made of; every crevice in her entire body and every pour oozed pure honest sweat. They each gave back what the other had given, tirelessly, persistently and oh so joyously was their passion shared as their night turned into day; and then reality! As Gloria tip toed down the stairway barefoot with her sandals in either hand she carefully opened the reception door and danced up the street to Mrs Kelly's and Julie.

'Well, well, did we have a good night?' said Julie sarcastically.

'Julie' as she stood with her back firmly against the door 'I think I'm in love……I am in love…..oh God but it's wonderful…….Julie Julie, I've never felt love like this before' and she slide down the door and sat staring into space.

'You're sick or else you really are in love! I go away for a week and this is what happens; what about me, who am I going to fall in love with!'

'You're a twice married woman Julie, what do you care about love you've had plenty!'

'Plenty of one-nighters but that's not love, I want the real thing and to wake up each morning with the same man beside me and to miss him every day until he comes home from work and for him to miss me every day while he's at work; someone who can't work thinking about me, can't concentrate for wanting to have me all to himself!' They held hands and Julie rested her head on Gloria's shoulder as best friends do in intimate moments of joy or sorrow; but in an instant the joy was shattered when Gloria remembered………..

It was about 9.30am when Glory B and Kelly came laughing up the stairs; they burst in expecting to find Julie and Gloria still fast asleep.

'Well, well, did we have a good night?' Julie said in that knowing it all tone of hers.

'Fabulous, just awesome, Julie……….you want to try it some time, you and mum!'

'Been there done that and have the T shirt' Julie laughed 'and also went back for seconds!'

'What about something to eat, I'm starving……..' and before Julie could finish the sentence Kelly burst in with news that shocked Julie to her polished toes.

'We've had breakfast and guess what……….a bus load of Russians stopped outside and came in for something to eat in the café……..the interpreter was telling us that they were all booked in to The Clarence and now because of the fire most of them are staying in the Belmont over in Ballyshannon and a few are staying next door in Maggie Sweeney's. You want to see them Julie, just up your street….handsome and muscles everywhere!'

Julie turned white. Her mouth fell open but nothing came out not even a lead me too them gag. She fell back and put her head below the pillow; Gloria and Glory B exchanged glances and laughed. Glory B guessed there was something of a Julie situation going on. What could it be this time she thought; then smiled and gave her mum a cheeky wink as she picked up a yellow napkin with the words SOUVENIR OF OUR WEDDING boldly printed around the edges and scrawled in the middle with red lipstick was a heart and the names Yuri & Julie xo.

'Don't you dare ask me anything! Gloria waved her hand indicating for the girls to leave.

The name Yuri sounded like an astronaut's name if Glory B remembered correctly, but where could Julie have met an astronaut; nothing was impossible if Julie was involved thought Glory B. The door slammed closed and to Julie it was like hearing in the distance a court room door being firmly closed and justice being served; a metaphor perhaps for what might be the consequences of Julie Marsden's drunken foolishness. She screamed from under the pillow 'I'm a wanted woman, get me out of here.' Gloria laughed so much she fell out of bed and just lay mesmerized by the absurdity that surrounded the whole situation. Suddenly out of nowhere Glory began to cry, her cry became sobs and the sobs became more sobs until she too grabbed her pillow and buried her head beneath it. She was going to die, and she just didn't want to face it, and neither did she want to share it with anyone; not Julie nor Henry but especial not Julie.

Chapter seventeen: Tough Choices

The final evening had arrived. Time was precious and passing too quickly for Gloria and Henry. At exactly 7pm everyone, including Ray, the garage man, was seated in the dining room of The Country House Hotel. Mrs Kelly looked gracious as she lit the tiny tee lights on every window ledge to heighten the sense of romance that she was creating with the soft lights and low music; she was a first class atmospherics expert and this was her stage where she performed her creative craft of match making of a kind.

Seated at the top of the table was Henry in his navy pinstriped suit. He wore neither tie nor shirt but instead a pale blue casual top and he was looking extra handsome, like a man in love and oozing sensuality. Next to Henry to his left sat Gloria, clad in very little. Her red silk top hung loose around her shoulders and showed quite a bit of cleavage when she moved her elbows on the table as she spoke to Henry in intimate whispers that Julie (seated next to Gloria) tried several times to ease-drop on, but to no avail as Ray (seated facing Julie) didn't seem to shut up much; he was newly fangled with the idea of being of interest to 'a young chick' though it maybe debateable as to whether Julie would have taken that as a compliment if she'd known that was how he thought of her...........but then again......

It was an oblong table covered with a beautiful pure white linen table cloth that another guest from another time had given to Mrs Kelly on her third stay at the hotel in appreciation for all her hospitality and friendship. The guest was another Belfast woman called Annie Walsh and she had obtained the table cloth years before when she worked in the linen mill off the Falls road; it was significant in a sort of way because it was the same Annie Walsh who recommended The Country House Hotel to Gloria or rather she recommended Mrs Kelly to her.

Then beside Ray and Julie sat Kelly and Gloria B who texted for most of the evening to each other and also to Peter and Rico who came in after the meal was over to bid their good byes to Gloria and Julie; they would see Henry tomorrow.

The music was turned up and the table cleared and the dancing began. First Julie tried to get the boys up before they left with the girls; but they were too in a hurry to be bothered with any messing around on the floor with Julie; so Julie and Ray led the dancing and surprisingly Ray was a good mover which impressed Julie so much it brought out her suggestive lip pursing and come to bed eying at him for the rest of the evening; unfortunately for Julie, Ray, though a good mover, was a little slow and rusty on the uptake; but Julie being Julie, like the Mounties, always gets her man. Ray didn't know it on the dance floor but he was in store for a few unexpected surprises in the back of his Lada, none of which he refused and all of which he enjoyed, it had been so long since he was intimate with a woman! But, the big question was, would Ray simply be another one of Julie's one-nighters? Ray didn't do one-nighters as Julie would soon discover; to her cost or to her pleasure would become apparent in the cold light of day!

Almost every episode in Gloria's life could be summed up with a song. A significant song of course, like: Nobody's Child, Leaving on a Jet Plane, You are my Sunshine, Stand by your Man and now moodying to If Tomorrow Never Comes in the bubble she and Henry had created seemed too real to be just a song, it was a truth that stung her heart.............it made her feel so sad but she could not share her secret sadness with Henry, in an instance she decided to leave first thing in the morning without saying goodbye; though tonight had not ended yet, it seemed to disappear so quickly. 'I love moodying with you Henry, you're a great moodier'

'Moodying, what's that when it's at home?'

'You honestly don't know! I'll have to teach you; it's what we're doing now, it's this slow dance'

'Oh, I didn't know we were dancing, I thought we were..............getting it on............' Henry nibbled at her ear as he whispered 'I thought this was a warm up to..............making love to you' they kissed passionately on the dance floor, the lights seemed to be spinning and suddenly the music ceased and passion had made them drunk. When their hungry lips broke reluctantly apart still not properly satisfied in that maze of emotion that new lovers encounter as one body pursuing not the exit, but the prolongation of isolation in this new sensual territory of awakening. Their kiss had lasted a life time and everyone else had gone, at least that's how it seemed; they didn't care, why would they, this was a new and unexpected world for Gloria and Henry.

Henry could not believe that this was happening to him. It was as though he had died and was reborn. In this instance he felt he was the happiest man in the world; what could go wrong for he knew that Gloria felt the same and love was stronger than both of them; it would not be possible to ignore. He had to make his proposal tonight. 'I'm not letting you go' he said and Gloria bit her lip as she turned away. 'Let's walk a bit outside and admire the sky and the river and the fields and love' he said as he held both her trembling hands. He smiled and winked at her and again, out of character, she felt embarrassed, her face reddened and she had to look away before she began to cry for the second time in 24 hours. 'Do I embarrass you? I don't mean to, it's just I feel we've so little time here that I have this need to be honest with you............I'm crazy about you, like some love sick teenager back home, I...................I think............I know I love you, I'm in love with you my Northern Rose you even make me say things like I don't normally say, you make me feel things that I've only dreamed of feeling, can't you see, I'm crazy just crazy about you.......I love you, honest, I do I love you' Henry winks again waiting on Gloria's reply.

Gloria's heart is pounding and the words I love you melt away all the anxiety that restrained her from telling him that she loved him too and she says the words softly and with passion 'Henry Dickson, I have never loved anyone this way before, I have never felt this happy in all my life, Henry.............I think I love you...........no, no I mean I love you...........I love you, I love you, a million times I love you, just let this night never end I love you. In her mind at this moment nothing at all mattered only Henry......... the tumour was forgotten about, for now at least, she was going to enjoy these last hours with Henry, the man she was in love with at this moment and if her life was to end in the morning then that would be fine, that's the way she was trying to reason this whole situation with Henry out because in the first place last week she didn't know she had a tumour and she didn't know either that she was about to meet the man of all her dreams in the form of Henry Dickson...........how else should she be thinking.

Henry stood up and held out his hands and said 'can I have this last dance with you'. Gloria stood up and straightened her mini skirt down a little and fell into Henry's open arms. His embrace was like angels spreading their wings around her lifting her effortlessly off the ground and taking her up to heaven. They didn't move, that is they didn't dance in motion but their hearts danced and bounced off one another and a new excitement and joy ran through their veins overwhelming their ability to move.

4am and dawn broke. They lay on the grass and the sweet smell of the honey-suckle that hung above them filled their senses with an appetite for serenity and more love. The peace was disturbed by the feeling that something was crawling up Gloria's neck, it was an early morning earwig; she jumped startling Henry but he managed to brush it from her neck before it reached her hair. So that was the indication that the night was over. They parted at the hotel and Henry strolled happily in to his own room for some rest and a shower after his wonderful night of love.

Gloria rushed to have a shower and packed faster than she ever did before; she had to get away on the first bus to Belfast at 7am before Henry would know she'd gone. She texted Glory B to find out where she was but discovered an earlier text from her daughter telling her that she was away for the next two days with Kelly, Peter and Rico on a gig. She had asked for her mums' permission but got no reply and so just went on, she knew it would be okay. Gloria was angry but in too much of a hurry to bother texting or ring Glory B at this hour. Speed was important at this stage. She wanted no one to see her go. In fact, as she rushed to the bus station she thought that this was another of those Julie moments that she experienced from time to time. But, this really was a life and death matter. Gloria was the only passenger on board; she sat at the back of the bus to look out at the sleeping Fundoran perhaps for the last time and wondered what Henry would say when he would find out that she'd gone. Her heart ached much worse than when she found out that Glory B's father didn't want to know her when she became pregnant. That aloneness, that feeling that you really are alone and rejected and when there is no one to share what you're going through, it's like falling out of an airplane with no parachute............not that she ever had fallen out of an airplane but she equated the fear of falling with the fear of not knowing how things with the tumour were going to end. Would there be inevitability, a certainty that she could not reach the ground without having to crash land?

Whatever was ahead, Gloria would have to face it alone. She was not going to burden Glory B unnecessarily; maybe it might come to that but only if she was completely powerless.

Chapter 18:
Back Home and Alone

There was a strangeness about turning the key in the door; it was as if this was no longer where she lived. She'd had a taste of a different world with Henry, with him everything just fell into place. Now, he was gone. Out of her life and she felt alone. This is all nonsense she thought acknowledging the fact that she only knew him a few days. How could your life change in such a short time how could someone else make such a difference to you? How? Love. Love makes everything seem new, different, worthwhile. Worth living for. But she walked away. Getting on that bus was the end of the line for Henry and Gloria. It was her decision, not his; he knew nothing about how coldly she was able to cut the 'him' out of 'them'. She had no idea just what she had done. She had bundled all that love up and threw it away. And poor Henry; he was on his way to having breakfast with her before seeing her to the bus station as he thought!

She lifted the mail from the hall floor leaving it beside the phone and noticing that there were quite a few messages as she turned the bleeper off and thought that that was a bit unusual because generally none of her friends left her messages because she never would get back to them anyway so there was no point in leaving Gloria a message. She kicked her case further up the hall, slammed the door behind her and walked back out into the Belfast sunshine. She walked like someone without a care in the world but her eyes told a different story. They betrayed her outer calmness and displayed a blankness that couldn't see beyond the outside of their sockets; there was a lifelessness about her and finally she just followed a group of kids from Clonard youth club into the Dunville park and sat on a bench that faced the Grosvenor Road and starred at the cars and lorries as they started and stopped at the traffic lights moving upwards towards the Springfield Road or left to the Falls Road or turning right and going down towards Divis Street and the city centre. She just stared, not seeing or feeling anything. Sometime later, an hour or so, she stood up and headed back home but changed her mind; walking up Clonard Street she went instead to the monastery. There was no one else there praying or lighting candles; she was alone and she was glad of the solitude. She had no change in her pocket and she lit a candle without paying, then sat in front of Our Lady's altar but prayer eluded her mind, she just sat there for some time, not thinking just being there, breathing big sigh-full breathes.

It was exactly 6pm when she arrived back home and the angelus bells began to ring as they always did from St Peter's. A comforting daily routine peel, but not today she didn't hear them ring; there was no comfort in anything anymore. She found herself upstairs lying on top of the bed frightened not remembering how she'd got there. Frightened of the tumour and frightened of what she had done to Henry. Her phone rang a few times but she ignored it. Sleep had forsaken her and in the morning she heard the postman deliver more letters, probably bills she thought.

Eventually after drifting in and out of light sleep she was startled by the thunder and gallops of feet on the stairs. Half dazed, Gloria turned to face the door when it burst open and her daughter ran and threw herself on top of the bed beside her. 'Mum, what happened, where did you get too we've been searching all night long for you'. Gloria fell back onto her pillow and began to sob. They both hugged and kissed and Gloria tried to talk but the words just didn't come out. 'I know it's hard for you but it's going to be hard for me as well, we're a team, you and I, we go through things together, not separately, not as individuals, we're a team, I'm part of you, you made me you give me life, mum don't shut me out...........I love you with all my heart' she put a kiss on her finger and held it to her mother's lips. Gloria sat up and asked about Henry. 'What did he say? Did he try to follow me? Where is he now? I think I really should have explained things to him..............I'm in love with him G.B.'

'G.B. you haven't called me that in years mum, I loved when you used to say 'quick G.B. tidy up and I'll get us a pizza, we'll have a girlie night in........... Girls just want to have fun........remember mum, we must have worn that video out, we played it so much; bet I can rake it out from under the stairs.............eh' she waited for approval..........'come on..........and I'll ring for a pizza up to Jeanie's, they deliver fast..........what do you think....................what are you thinking'?

Gloria pulled the shower curtain across the length of the bath, turned on the hot water and waited for the spray to soak her hair and neck and back as she stood naked and calm before turning around to let its gushing force help relieve her inner turmoil; at least that was her plan, but, there was no bathroom fragrance to carry her off to that other place in her mind; shower gel and soap were still suit cased and the smell of the lemon plant on the window ledge only reminded Gloria of the orphanage. Why does everything in my life go wrong; that very thought had just run through her head when the bathroom door burst open and the shower curtain was pulled of its rail (accidently) falling in slow motion to the rim of the bath and Gloria yelling.........'What what's wrong now..........what's happened......'? Glory B had a sheet of paper in her hand, her mouth opened and she handed the sheet to Gloria in her complete nakedness with the shower still spraying water and soaking the page. She couldn't think straight, she turned her back to the shower so she could read the page. It was a letter, as she read it she sat down in the bath, Glory B turned the shower off and put a towel around her mum's shoulders and waited for the expected yells of relief or anger or rage or WHAT! 'WHAT.......what does this mean.......a mistake...............a mistake..............the wrong patient.............or the right patient the wrong letter......... Oh My God...............I'm free, I'm alive I'm not going to die.........I have no tumour it was all a dream a mistake........ How? How? How?' Glory B sat on the edge of the bath and hugged her mum accidently sliding down on top of her, they both laughed in an outrageous manner that finally became roars and screeches of pain relief that was being emptied from somewhere deep within their being; just before they managed to get up out of the bath the shower squirted one big blast of crystal clear water over them both. It was like a double baptism; the beginning, perhaps, of something new, perhaps.

There was nothing left of the pizza and garlic dip; as Gloria put the empty containers into the bin she stalled and gazed up at the moon and the stars. She recognised Venus and the Starry Plough, the stars weren't so numerous in Belfast as they were in Donegal, something to do with the reflection of city lights Henry had told her that night by the river............she felt so good even to think about Henry, her blood felt warm and alive. Before she closed the back door she looked up at the sky one last time and whispered a prayer asking God and the universe to send Henry back into her arms, somehow; she also said a prayer for whom ever the doctor had mixed her file up with and who would now know the bad news that they had a tumour. 'Amen' she whispered softly to the sky and the stars seemed to twinkle back at her as if to let her know that they had heard her gentle prayer.

Gloria would discover tomorrow when she returned to Fundoran that Henry and Kelly were on their way home to Boston; but at least there was good news from a surprising quarter. Ray had taken a real fancy to Julie and he just wasn't going to let her walk out of his life that easily. His garage which was opened every day and night of the week remained unmanned and a sign which read 'Gone to bed,(but not to sleep) be back sometime' was stuck on the corrugated iron door that didn't have a lock fitted as there was never a need to lock anything in it up.

Their every waking moment together was spent sure enough in Ray's four poster bed. He had good taste for a man on his own and Julie was already making plans to decorate the bathroom!!! She'd always wanted a Jacuzzi and now she'd found the man who would get her one; she giggled into Rays somewhat hairy ear 'Oh lá lá' which, she wasn't quite sure meant, but she did make it sound suggestive to Ray's untrained but sensual eardrum. 'Oh lá lá anything for you darling' he interjected with a slightly Americanised tone to his Donegal accent and that was just before he reached under the bed for something, as though it had been rehearsed (at least in his mind) a prop, placed not by accident but in anticipation to be worn at the appropriate moment of moments, yes, you're right, it was a cowboy hat with tassels. That four poster bed had never known such fun in all its years. There was no chance of Julie returning to Belfast just now, even though it would mean that she'd lose her job in the dry cleaners. But what the heck, Julie was a survivor and now she had hit the jackpot with a financial catch like Ray. Not that he was rich but he was richer than anyone else that Julie had had an affair with; what he lacked in good looks he definitely made up for in the bedroom. But really, even at this early stage, Julie knew he was a good man, and a great catch for her.

Henry didn't leave any forwarding address. He was devastated Mrs Kelly told Gloria when she showed him the note. She had to show it because he thought something worse had happened to her. He and Kelly left immediately without returning to say good-bye to Mrs Kelly. She watched as they packed their cases into the taxi that had been waiting for over ten minutes with the meter running. Joe Sweeny the taxi driver told Mrs Kelly on his return that they went straight to Dublin airport and barely spoke the whole journey.

Gloria had to do something to get Henry back into her life; he was too wonderful to go on without. She was in love. She was this crazy woman in love and she had to get her man back where he belonged, in her arms; but how, that was the problem. She went home to Belfast a determined woman. Then finally, she had a brainwave.

Chapter 19:
Floating like a butterfly
and stung by a bee

THREE MONTHS LATER

The weeks dragged in and Gloria could not bear to listen to any music that would remind her of Henry and Fundoran; Leonard Cohen was depressing her and she was coaxed into joining the fitness club in the Falls Leisure Centre, she did have a few brighter moments with her instructor Homer, but then he had a heart attack and that put the lid on her self-help efforts. Gloria felt lost, out on a limb and she did something she never thought she'd do; she'd do a Julie. She'd go hunting. Man hunting!

Gloria used the same technique as Henry in her desperate quest to find where she belonged. She employed the help of Mrs Jess from the Credit Union who never let the fact of not knowing someone to stand in the way of her inquisitive mind; there were nearly two hundred on the internet. It was a laborious task but she enjoyed every click of the mouse for this was not her first encounter with paving the path of true love. Mrs Jess crafted a plausible email to each parish office in the Boston diocese hoping that someone would know Henry or Kelly and get back to her with an address or cell number. However, very few returned her enquiry. She also thought of putting an advertisement in each bulletin but decided against that idea when a small charge was required.

Then out of sheer good fortune Mrs Jess keyed into her Packard Bell the words: Henry and Kelly Dickson Boston Ballyshannon Donegal Ireland; and an obituary popped up in the Boston Herald with the matching words. 'Good God' Mrs Jess said aloud 'is he dead or what?' She quickly scrolled down the page at first missing the names then on her way up she found the memorial notice: 'O'Neill Roslín and Moira great aunts to Henry Dickson: died one day apart. May they rest in peace forever. Funeral in Ireland. Mass offered in St Patricks Parish Church BROCKTON 10am. September 26th. Henry and Kelly Dickson. Mary Queen of the Gael pray for them.

Mrs Jess pushed a loan through first thing next morning. Without any good byes Gloria waited at the airport with just a rucksack and a mind that was made up! She didn't intend staying in Boston; she was going to make a statement short and simple I love you Henry Dickson and that was it. She would go knock Henry's door and then…… whatever……….. . She kept asking herself things like………what if Henry hesitates, if he shows any signs of a change of heart what would she do? She would follow her instincts of course; if it didn't feel right she would turn on her heel and walk away. Her return ticket was non-refundable; flying out on the Friday and returning home on the Monday she could stretch what little money she had if everything went as she had hoped it would. She had been so foolish to let him go and now there was a price to be paid……..but could her heart afford the cost?

It was a seven hour flight to New York and security at the airport was very tight. Gloria was pulled over and brought into a room where her rucksack was searched and she had to give an account of what she was doing in America. She was fascinated by all the attention and she willingly spilled out her whole story but for some reason the security people didn't believe her. After repeating it a few times Gloria started to doubt herself; this was definitely a Julie situation and there was no doubt about that!

The facts were: Gloria came to America to find a man who called himself Henry after knowing him for only a matter of days and had had no contact with him since. She didn't have an address or cell number for him but assumes he is the author of the memorial in a print-out from a web page on Mrs Jess's computer back at her local Credit Union in Belfast and now she has been detained by security in New Yonkers airport and is starting to get a little worried. The security are particularly interested in why Gloria doesn't have any luggage; they have suggested that perhaps she intends to take a lot more back to Ireland than she's brought out. Gloria doesn't have a political bone in her body and doesn't get where all the questioning is going! However, everything will soon become crystal clear!

'How many passports do you own, Gertrude?' the nice security man asked her smiling as though he'd known Gloria all his life. 'ONE, off course, just the one, that's it there in your hand'

'That's right Gertrude' this is your passport, your Irish issued passport, but we're not talking about your Irish passport, it's the other one we're interested in, you know the one you were using 6 months ago when you gained entry into Cuba'

'Cuba' she gulps. 'I've never been outside Ireland in my whole entire life, ever'

'Well, you got this passport 8 years ago and you've never used it, is that what you're telling me, Gertrude'?

Gloria spoke so fast it was hard for the nice security man to pick up on what she was saying. 'Yes, that's right, you see, around that time I'd hoped that I'd get a claim or win something in the lottery and be able to go to Nashville instead of Fundoran for the country music, I'm into country in a big way, my best friend Julie went to Nashville this year, though that's another story, so you see, I always had hopes of visiting America, but financially just couldn't afford it'

'Until now, Gertrude?'

'Well, not really, you see I had to borrow the money from the Credit Union, Mrs Jess was really helpful, I didn't think she could be so considerate'

'Slow down Gertrude I think I'm going to need an interpreter'.

'Oh please, don't call me by that name, it's not my real name' she naively stated. The nice security man looked a little shocked and sat down beside Gloria, in fact it looked like he was about to put his arm around her when the female security person quickly responded 'got you misses, travelling under a false name and that's only for starters, now, who is your contact here, who are you meeting?' her tone quickly softened when she made eye contact with the nice security man; 'tell us now and we can go get them or him or her whoever it is you're supposed to meet, and clear this whole matter up and you can go on and enjoy your stay here in the U.S.A. Okay Gerturde?' Gloria was becoming a little confused by this line of questioning; she was telling the truth about her name, she hated that name but it was on her birth certificate and the only compromise the nuns in the orphanage reached with her was to cut it short to Gertie; she tried to persuade them to call her Gloria, which she thought was a most beautiful name one Christmas after hearing the nuns sing Gloria in excelsis deo; always trying to ingratiate herself in the orphanage never paid off much; to be an orphan was to be always the outsider, and that had only disadvantages.

'My name's Gloria, Gloria Jenkins, my surname is real, it's just I never liked being called Gertrude and then Gertie for short was worse because it rhymed with garters; in the orphanage the other kids called me Gertie garters and I hated it'

'Orphanage, look Gertrude, we're not interested in your whole life history, it's just from 6 months ago when you came over to Cuba via United States and left through Canada...........now tell us all about it. Is Henry Dickson your contact here, did he take you to meet anyone before you left for Cuba?'

They seemed to ignore just about everything Gloria was telling them, she couldn't sense them into the truth that she was over in Boston trying to find the man she loved. Henry Dickson. It seemed like hours since this saga began and Gloria was on melt down. She was tired and frightened. She had been stripped and put into a holding cell wearing some sort of an issued jumpsuit. All her possessions had been confiscated. Things were looking pretty dim from inside the cell. Then out of nowhere a glimmer of light appeared in the form of her Irish passport. Someone, perhaps some kind security person believed her and had contacted the Irish Embassy in New York.

Standing on the other side of the bars stood a red cheeked, blond haired man in his forties, sort of heavy looking but carried his weight with grace because of his height, possibly over six feet and dressed in a double breasted Armani dinner suit. 'Hi' he smiled, 'don't look so frightened, everything is going to get sorted, I'm here to begin that process now..................open up guard' he spoke with authority and a familiarity that he'd been here before.............many times as it turned out; he greeted Gloria warmly with a firm handshake and held her hands in his for a moment or two. 'I'm here on behalf of the Irish Consulate, we were just notified an hour or so ago that you were here and in trouble.........as you see I was on my way to an Embassy dinner.....I'm not missing much so don't be overawed by my appearance. Now, from the beginning' he sat on the chair beside the single bed in the tiny cell opening his brief case..........' By the way I'm Charlie Townsend and you are....................?

'I'm Gloria Jenkins from Belfast'

'Now, is that your name................is it? They said there's some confusion as to your real or proper name, is that correct?................I have to get this out of the way before we can see what the real problem is, so don't be afraid of me..............be yourself and relax and above all I can only help you if you're honest with me, no shit, honesty is the only thing I respond to in this game! I've seen it all here in this cell: good girls gone bad and bad girls gone good. How's that for a conundrum?' Gloria merely acknowledged this suited funny man with a nervous smile. She wasn't used to the American ease when dealing with serious matters like hers!! Much of what Charlie was saying went over Gloria's head and the reality of her predicament was slowly sinking in. After telling him all about Henry and her 'tumour' she was beginning to doubt herself. After telling her story a few times it sort of didn't ring true anymore. She began to feel a little uneasy about what she was doing in America at all.   Now all these years later Gloria was right back in the orphanage and to reinforce that emotional backward journey, the security people were still calling her Gertrude. Charlie had promised to contact Glory B first thing in the morning, which would be the afternoon in Belfast. Gloria knew her daughter would get in touch with a solicitor or someone who would know what to do and as long as Julie wasn't told then Gloria wouldn't have to worry about Julie coming out to rescue her, because, she might not be allowed back into the U.S.A. herself; after all, even Julie didn't know exactly what she had got up to in Nashville and Vegas.

There was a stone silence all night. To Gloria the unnatural stillness of this isolated environment was scary. Not a single sound or creek or anything that gave the impression of life anywhere within this cell was heard. Gloria thought they had forgotten she was there but at 7am the outer door opened and then the cell door and a smiling security person brought her in some breakfast. The guard was friendly and asked if she'd slept well and also told her she'd take her to the wash room when she finished eating, to freshen up. 'Charlie's a nice guy, he'll be back later today and maybe something can be sorted........ But.............if you've did something you shouldn't have done, we'll get you.........got it......but don't be afraid, I've a good instinct about people who try to do our country wrong and I don't think you would.........chin up as the British say..............oh I forgot you're Irish aren't you?............ what's the equivalent then to 'chin up' in Ireland?'

'I suppose it's something like........'God bless or maybe keep the faith'..........I'm not really sure even if we have an equivalent. We've our own language, though I can't speak it.........more's the pity, I tried for years but just gave up in the end. Gloria shrugged her shoulders and took a deep, deep sigh afraid to think what the day might bring, for instance, maybe there would be some other wild accusation against her maybe this other girl had left a trail that would make Gloria look guilty even though it would have to be proven that she'd broken the law................oh God, she thought what a mess, even Julie has never been arrested; though that, she knew was more down to luck than anything else.

One o'clock, then two o'clock, then three o'clock, four, five, six o'clock and the cell door opened wide and there like the mythical warrior, Cuchulain, stood Henry Dickson head and shoulders higher than Charlie and the security guard. Gloria was speechless as she leapt to her feet, feeling that her heart was about to fly out through her mouth, it was beating so fast at the sight of Henry. He winked that wonderful wink that she loved so much then drew her so tight she felt the rhythm of the nerves that pulsated through his body and she longed for his kiss to soothe everything into place and make this terrible mistake go away.

The embrace lasted longer than the security guard approved and so Charlie suggested they all be seated to discuss what may or may not be about to happen. Henry held Gloria's hand caressing it with his thumb giving her a feeling that two parallel worlds were taking place. The wonderful world of being with the man she loved with all her heart (she was certain of this now beyond doubt) and then this other world that was nothing short of a nightmare...........she wondered which would became her reality......!

'Right people, this is the situation as I see it' he stated with conviction. 'Gloria, you've been detained by immigration security and may be charged with trying to enter the country illegally using a false passport. Now, the thing is, they know you're not using a false passport........... right.............but...............they can hold you on that if you don't cooperate and give them any information on who used your I.D. 6 months ago with the British passport..........understand........they believe she was involved in either securing arms from a known arms dealer or in the shipment of laundered money for a drugs cartel from Cuba.............now the thing is Gloria........how come this person uses your I.D. without you knowing......they would have needed certain information and documents from you.........the immigration people want to know how come...........understand............. and then you tell them your real name is Gertrude and not Gloria..............so you can see where the department is coming from can't you?' The whole time Charlie was speaking the security lady was analysing Gloria's body language.................her conclusion was fairly accurate, Gloria was crazy. Crazy about Henry. Madly in love in fact. It was so obvious. And the same could be deduced from Henry's body language. He was a man in love with the woman whose hand he was caressing and protecting.

Gloria repeated her story again and this time it was to Henry. Charlie and the security person left them alone while they both went into the adjoining room to observe as the other security people were already observing through the two-way mirror, that was so obvious, even Gloria knew they were being watched from the other side of it. Henry wasted no time in proclaiming his undying love for Gloria.............'I'll wait for you forever' he joked as he pulled her as close as he could to his beating heart and they slowly tasted and kissed and quietly moaned like secret lovers do because they know that this opportunity may never come again.

'What do you think?' Charlie asked Nick who was head of security: a small lean bald man with one chocolate brown eye and one blue eye; what are the changes of such a coincidence as this occurring; well lucky for Gloria Nick understood heterochromia, the eye condition that changes the colour of one eye, otherwise security would most certainly have investigated the possibility of Gloria wearing eye contacts to disguise her appearance and then losing one of them. Luckily that was one line of inquiry she didn't have to endure; she and Nick had the same eye condition though Gloria's was genetic and Nicks developed after an injury during his military service in the '60's. Nick had a stern look about him, someone a captive wouldn't want to mess with because his body language gave nothing away, there was an air of unpredictability about him, he was known as the tough guy in the department. He'd made a name for himself during the Vietnam War and got a medal for bravery during the Battle of Hill 937 or as it was later renamed; Hamburger Hill. So he definitely wouldn't be a time waster for the sake of it; he would want results that were watertight and permanent; Charlie had a lot of respect for Nick because he basically knew he was an honest guy.

'She's not smart enough to be a good liar' he replied

with his eyes fixed on Gloria through the mirror. 'But courageous enough to come here on her own with just a name, and crazy enough to search for this guy who she only knew for a few days, so in my opinion for what it's worth is, that the danger here, is in the fact she's an idealist.............a dreamer........a crazy dreamer........... this is like a fairy-tale to that woman.......her dream is our nightmare' he shrugged his bony little shoulders and looked Charlie straight in the eyes. 'We'll show her the photo shots of the girl with her passport and see if she comes up with a name, we don't think this other girl is from Belfast but we might have a lead to a place called Sligo'.

Dramatically the cell door banged open echoing like gun shots down the corridor and shocking Henry and Gloria into letting go of one another. A brave sigh of relief streamed from Gloria as Charlie headed the charge with the good news that she was believed by immigration security. He explained that it was vital for her to try and identify the other girl using her British passport. Firstly Gloria closed her eyes when presented with the stills of the fraudster for she was frightened that she may know the girl and that would bring more complications into her life when she would return to Belfast; then when commanded by the Nick boy, to open her eyes and look, she obeyed sheepishly and was relieved to discover that she'd never seen this girl in her life before.

The episode dramatically ended as swiftly as it had begun. Security agreed that Gloria was not a risk to the National Security of the U.S.A.so they were freeing her if she agreed to take the next flight home. She would have to board immediately. What could she do to get staying longer with Henry? There seemed no solution that was within reach at this moment. She turned to Henry and seeing him whisper something to Charlie she surmised it was for advice on what course of action they could take (she was pretty confident now that it was they and not just her) in all this confusion she felt a warmth that cloaked her making her feel safe once more.

Charlie lifted his cell phone off the table and began keying something in and when he finished he nodded to Henry and the most unexpected and magical thing happened. All eyes were on Gloria. Joe Dolan singing 'More and More' blasted from the phone, immediately Gloria was transported back to when she and Henry met. How could she not love him more now, than she did then; so much and yet so little had happened between them in this short time. As the song played Henry got down on one knee and taking Gloria's shaking hand in his he kissed it. First he looked into her blue eye and then her brown eye and said 'Before you escape again, will you marry me Gloria, I love you, my northern rose'. Everyone was silent, Joe Dolan belting out more and more and more I want you near me, more and more....................no one heard the song anymore as they waited on Gloria's answer. Gloria yelled 'you're crazier than I am.........Henry Dickson..........I love you........you mad, mad man.....I love you' Then the entire room applauded as Henry held Gloria and they kissed; Charlie, Nick and the security woman quickly turned away to give them that little piece of privacy that lasted a few seconds. 'When and where?' Gloria laughed.

'Here and now if that's possible' said Henry looking at Charlie for some sort of legal clarification. Charlie in turn said 'It's not impossible, but Nick this is your department, immigration can work wonders I'm told................try to remember what it's like to be young and in love Nick.............' Nick smirked in Henry's direction; obviously not concurring with the suggestion that Henry looked that young. But still, he thought, love is love and age just doesn't count; in that instant Nick's thoughts were well disguised for he was a lonely man, someone that love never was kind to; he even felt slightly enviously of Henry; from his days with the Military he had disciplined his emotions so it was hard for anyone to get close to him; now strangely he felt bemused by this whole situation for it was new to Nick; he'd thought he'd heard it all but somehow, Gloria brought a memory from somewhere; not a picture memory but a gut feeling from deep in Nicks past, maybe his childhood, into the fore. There was something innocent something good, deep down, about the situation and Nick had never come across anything like this before in his career with the department. He had dealt with the lowest of the low through his job and it was never without danger but this particular case was different. He decided to himself that he would help Gloria if he could. But, it had to be now otherwise it would be too late.

Chapter 20:
Back Home...............again!

She was so tired that all she wanted to do was sleep but as the plane made its fourth attempt to take off and failing yet again, sleep was the last thing she needed if she was to be the first up the aisle to the emergency door should things get any worse.

Gloria thought to herself that Henry would be watching; he wouldn't have left the airport until he saw her fly off into the clouds. She was not to know that indeed he'd left immediately after he kissed her good-bye as the security ushered her through the departure doors. He was in a hurry, after all, to break the new to Kelly..............and Cathy.............yes that's right, Cathy, who he had married and who ran off with that rotten pig of a gardener, Deano Rodgers. Cathy never thought that Henry would ever be rich and that was the main reason she divorced him so soon after leaving him. She really believed that she would make it big time in the film industry and that wasn't her only disappointment either. She never did marry Deano, because as it turned out he was already married five times and never once divorced. So while he was doing time and it became apparent that Cathy was no Marilyn Monroe she drifted from one location to another without success or fulfilment and eventually made her way back to Boston and to Henry because she knew he was a decent man and would help her out until she could make other arrangements.......again. Kelly, well that's another story, she was like Henry's guard dog, she barked as loudly as she could to frighten Cathy from trying to get back into Henry's bed. But there was no chance of that in any case, as far as Henry was concerned, because he knew he loved Gloria and was crossing the Atlantic after Christmas to find her.........again.

Henry had a lot to tell Gloria but it could wait for a while longer; especially now that they had just become husband and wife. Yes you heard right; husband and wife. As it turned out Nick was a good guy and a closet romantic. Back at the airport in the holding cell next to Gloria's and by an odd coincidence, there was a Justice Of The Peace waiting to be interviewed, it was something about smuggling ladies from another country into America for arranged marriages and as luck had it he was licensed to perform marriage ceremonies. Charlie acted as witness and the security lady, with Nick's permission got some newly shredded paper from a waste bin in the next office to throw on the newlyweds and make the occasion look slightly authentic. After the I do's and before the Kiss, Gloria bravely spoke up saying 'I would like to say something for Henry, my husband, and this is it, because I know you only know one poem of by heart, I want to confess that I also only know one poem by heart and it means so much to me because it was my mother's favourite, she just loved Yeats and so I've always treasured these words and I've never said them to anyone before, and now I feel it fitting, for want of a better word, to say them to you Henry, I know you'll understand how much they mean to me ....' looking into his eyes she slowly almost in a whisper recited 'Had I the heavens' embroidered cloths, enwrought with golden and silver light, the blue and the dim and the dark cloths of night and light and the half-light, I would spread the cloths under your feet: but I, being poor, have only my dreams; I have spread my dreams under your feet; tread softly because you tread on my dreams'. Henry pulled her close amid the round of applause and confetti of sorts. He knew that Gloria understood him, and he loved her for that and for much more.

Kelly was elated with the news, to have Gloria and Glory B in their lives permanently was the icing on the cake after being told two weeks previously that she and Henry were going to move home from Boston to Donegal to River

Cottage. Great Aunts Moira and Roslin had left Henry the cottage and surrounding land in their will. Rico was also a beneficiary; he was left plenty of shares in a thriving business and lots of money besides. Now, he would go without delay to Brazil and work on the building project for the street kids there, with Fr Hanna; maybe Kelly would join them for Rico had been a source of inspiration to Kelly since her return back to Boston. She had been tempted a few times to get in touch with him, but, the blood tie kept putting her off.

Cathy, well Cathy would go quietly. Henry was his usual sensitive self as he broke the news to her that he had married someone whom she knew nothing about. She did take it well and as always had her own contingency play. You see, since her return to Boston she reassumed her twice weekly appointments in Stefan's Hair and Beauty Salon and quickly re-established herself as his top model. The arrangement worked quite well considering that now his clientele had aged and also the ratio between his female clients and his male clients had about evened and the male clients were willing to pay more for beauty treatment................!

There was no clapping or cheers as the plane lifted upwards towards the heavens. All the passengers strapped in to their seats and holding on to the chair arms like grim death were now more afraid to be in the air than they were to be on the ground. It was a terrifying experience, but especially for anyone who already had a fear of flying. The lady sitting next to Gloria was from Bangor and she had moved from the middle aisle seats over to where she now sat shaking and holding on to Gloria's right arm. When the lady tried to speak she covered her mouth with her left hand to hide her missing set of dentures. The missing lower set caused her to speak with a severe lisp. Gloria learned from the lady's husband, who was obviously of pension age and hard of hearing that his wife had had words with him earlier before take-off, probably due to nerves and her fear of flying. He recounted three times what had led to the loss of the dentures; 'it was a complete fluke' he kept saying and at the end of each account he would look at his wife for her approval of his version of the event, but no approval was acknowledged; instead only the dirtiest of looks accompanied with mumbled lisping words that sounded like obscenities and threats to the poor man even after he went back like a little dejected puppy to his basket to lick his wounds.

Seven hours was too long a time to pretend to be asleep, so when the food came around that was Gloria's chance to excuse herself and to explore the plane away from the

Bangor lady. She had a great time saying hello to so many people with so many different accents; Gloria thought to herself 'this is the life for me; I should have been a pilot'!!!!

Once again all the passengers braced themselves; this time for the landing. It was a strange thought that struck Gloria, for one reason, and that was because there was so much depth to it; not that Gloria was really a shallow girl but she usually kept the deep thinking stuff out of bounds for she was not easily given to pessimism. But the thought struck her like lightning. What if she were to die this minute with all this happiness and joy she had in her heart, where would it go? Would it be lost? Could she take it with her to where ever she would end up; she shivered and took a deep sigh and prayed a prayer to her guardian Angel.........whom she hadn't prayed to in years. It would be awful, she thought, if she were to die now when she was finally happy. She shook herself and the negativity out from wherever it had sprung. Taking a deep breath she did what all other the passengers were doing and held like grim death onto the arms of her seat. Five, four, three, two, one....................we've landed.........the shouts and cheers went up then the clapping...........'There now........it wasn't too bad' said the Bangor lady to Gloria without the lisp because her husband had found or rather an air hostess had the dentures pointed out to her by the grandmother of a little boy who found them under his seat (only a grandmother would understand the need for dentures to be returned, perhaps) so all was well with the Bangor couple for now anyway and Gloria thought to herself how amazing things turn out if you're blessed with a good set of dentures!!! Sighs of relief went up when the plane came to a complete stand-still. Home sweet home now for Mrs Gloria Dickson; and she wasn't the only one with good news.

Chapter 21:
Weddings are like Buses

Mrs Jess just happened to call to find out how Boston was going when the phone call came from Charlie giving the good news that Gloria was safely on her way back home and would be arriving in Dublin, not Belfast, as was hoped, at 11pm that night. Glory B was happy that her mum would soon be home but had planned to get the bus from outside the Europa Hotel in town to go to the International Airport to meet her there whenever she would get the call; now the bus journey to and from Dublin would take hours. It was fortunate that Mrs Jess had called and she kindly offered Glory B a lift. 'Sure, my car's outside love, I was only going to bingo in St John's tonight and I can get Kitty McGettigan to play a couple of books for me, sure I'd do the same for Kitty, come on, get your coat on and we'll head up to Ballymurphy to see Kitty first. Okay........ that's us then, hope you made sure the back door is locked, don't want Gloria coming home to a an empty house!'

'Mum is right about you Mrs Jess, you really do think of everything!' And off they drove to Ballymurphy and then to the M1 where Mrs Jess was showing signs of road rage. It was at Newry that a distraught Glory B realised that Mrs Jess was having difficulty seeing properly. 'I thought you wore glasses Mrs Jess, at least any time I was in the Credit Union you were wearing glasses, isn't that right?' Without stopping for a breath Mrs Jess explained: 'Well, you see dear, I'm long sighted and I usually do wear my glasses for reading and for driving, but, you know wee Marie Thompson from Springview Street, well, she was in paying off her loan and she was telling me that I should get contact lenses and it might take the years off me and sure enough it did. But, they are a bit hard to get used to you know, I must have lost one there coming away from Kitty's house because I haven't been able to see too well out of my left eye since we drove down the Whiterock Road, what do you think of that?'

'You mean you're driving with only one eye............... holy cow Mrs Jess, you'll get us both killed!' At that exact moment, the blur from headlights and the loud startling hunk of the horn from an oncoming lorry caused Mrs Jess to turn the wheel so quickly to the left that the car crashed up onto the footpath halting quickly due to the thickness of a Hawthorn bush that up until now had been the home of six young robins that Mrs Jess had now orphaned. Their mother who had been nursing a broken wing and was not alert enough to escape before the impact of the car destroyed her and their home; they were now in the blink of an eye both orphaned and homeless.................... poor birdies!!! Now not only was Mrs Jess seeing with one eye but the headlight on the left side of the car was smashed to bits and it now seemed impossible that they could continue their journey to Dublin airport in time to meet Gloria's flight...............but all was not lost.

It was another strange coincidence that had led Julie and Ray to be driving along that same stretch of road that in a way also involved Mrs Jess and this is how it came about.

A few days earlier Mrs Jess was on her tea break at the Credit Union and she religiously read the Irish News every single morning and could have told every single customer the names of everyone who had died from the Falls Road or who had moved from the parish of St Paul's or St Peter's and was now dead; currently that is. She felt that she was providing vital information to anyone who wasn't up to date with the local deaths; anyway, last Saturday morning, there was no Irish News and Mrs Jess read from cover to cover the Irish Times after refusing her boss's copy of The Sun............ and on the back page she noticed in bold type and capital letters the name JULIE LAMBETH, and she read with disbelief at first, but finally thinking that the coincidence of the name and the dates matching was too much not to be Julie who came in every year to get a loan for the summer holidays and for Christmas; Julie, Gloria's friend from Beechmount.

At one thirty that afternoon, Mrs Jess was standing outside Julie's door and lucky enough Julie had just arrived back from Donegal and was surprised to see Mrs Jess, at first Julie thought that she was round to tell her she was in arrears or something like that but then she remembered that she hadn't borrowed this year and had paid back in full her Christmas load. What could that auld doll want here, Julie thought as she watched her through the window getting out of her car; Julie waited before deciding whether or not to open the door to her. On the door step Mrs Jess took the Irish Times from her bag and began reading the advert to Julie; pulling her in by the arm in shock horror it wasn't long before Julie was in a panic. The advert read: Seeking the whereabouts of one Mrs Julie Putina formally MISS JULIE LAMBETH originally from Ireland was recently married in U.S.A. whereabouts currently unknown. If you know the whereabouts of the above person please contact: McMarshal Solicitors Grafton Street Dublin phone 003531 382222 or email: mcmarshal@erocon.ireland as soon as possible. A small reward offered.

Mrs Jess searched Julie's face as the sweat broke out

across it and Julie muttered an unrepeatable few words that usually Mrs Jess would not tolerate but in this instant she felt it was reasonable. Mrs Jess walked Julie into her compact kitchen. She had to pull a chair out and physically help Julie sit down.

'Do you want to tell me about it, Julie?'

Julie couldn't speak she just cried and Mrs Jess was mystified and also slightly upset for Julie. This caring side to Jean Jess was a bit of a surprise to the three girls, Gloria, Glory B and now Julie who knew her only through the Credit Union. She handed Julie a cup of tea with four spoons of sugar in it, stirred well and plenty of milk; with the first sip Julie thought she was going to be sick but after that it did calm her down, she stopped shaking at least. 'Now sweetheart, tell Aunt Jean what this is all about, don't be afraid, I promise, right hand up to God, I'll not tell a living soul if you don't want me to. Now come on........spit it out girl tell your Aunt Jean all about it'.

'What am I going to do Mrs Jess, I've done something really foolish and I'm going to be in big trouble for it...............maybe with the FBI even!

Mrs Jess laughed and put her arm around Julie and told her to close her eyes if it made it easier to say exactly what it was all about................She laughed even harder when

Julie finished telling her the whole story or at least what she remembered of it.............. 'And what's his name, did you even get his name before you married him?'

''Well when I saw the marriage certificate I think his name was something like Yuri, you know like your man who went into space............' they both laughed and Mrs Jess remarked 'Oh yeah, I think I know who you're talking about...........he bends spoons as well you know! But, Julie, let's be straight here, you know, they can't come all the way from America to arrest you for being drunk when you decided to marry a complete stranger.........now can they...............there's got to be more to it than this?' Julie decided to tell Mrs Jess the whole story that she was already married, for want of a better way of putting it, but was never divorced..............She waited for the shock on her new friends face but it never came. Mrs Jess, had a few secrets of her own, and could understand perfectly what Julie was going through............there were things from Jean Jess's younger days, before she was married, that she wouldn't be telling Julie about and hoped and prayed that no one would ever find out or she might lose her job in the Credit Union. It involved a court case in Birmingham in the sixties where Jean was charged with shoplifting and was given a three month prison sentence because it wasn't her first time. It was a nightmare for Jean but she learned then never to judge unless you've been there yourself and so that was why she'd taken a motherly interest in both girls, she liked them and they reminded her of herself in some ways at least. Now, back to the Newry Road on that particular night, Julie was returning from the solicitors' office in Dublin and was being driven by Ray, who had proposed to Julie four nights before; and she had accepted! She had never in her entire life been so head over heels in love; and at the same time happy. But, yesterday it seemed to be going to fall apart, just like always for Julie. Mrs Jess, after bringing the paper round to Julie's house agreed to get in touch with the solicitor by email first thing the next morning; Julie didn't surf! The appointment was made for the following day. Mrs Jess pretended to be Julie's mother but Tony McMarshalls' secretary wouldn't divulge what the advert was about. The news of the appointment was instantly relayed to Julie via mobile.

Julie had to tell Ray the whole story; I mean the whole story from start to finish about her two marriages. He didn't flinch an eye lid; after all, Ray was a lot older than Julie and had a predisposition to be able to judge characters well. All he said to Julie was 'What's past is past; we can't undo it, just live now like this is our only time together, our time, and no one else's time'. Julie marvelled at the wisdom pouring out of this garage man's mouth, and he was her man, and no one else's; and it felt so good.

What was to unfold in the offices of McMarshall's Solicitors was so incredible that Julie was dumb-struck. Yes, dumb-struck. It transpired that she, Julie Putin (nee Lambert) was now a widow and her late husband Yuri Putin had died by accident. Poor Yuri was hit and killed by a truck while running from a casino in Las Vegas with a cheque for one million dollars which he'd just won after gambling his last twenty dollars in a gaming machine. Julie was his next of kin; apparently the investigators could find no other living relatives. Julie was sole heir to his fortune. In the utopia at the solicitors office Julie confessed she'd no proof of the marriage because she ate the marriage certificate. It was a relief to be told that it must have been a copy of the certificate because Yuri had the original in his wallet. 'Thank God, he was a careful man then' Julie told or asked Tony McMarshall. McMarshall, sat with his elbows on his desk nursing his chin with clenched fists as he observed Julie's reaction to all this and not once did she show any signs of sorrow. She refrained from telling McMarshall just how long she'd know Yuri, for really she didn't know the answer to that herself, though at a guess, it could not have been more than three days.

After signing the required documents Julie and Ray walked out of Grafton Street a lot faster than they had walked in. When they reached Ray's car he unlocked the passenger door for Julie and as she got in to the seat he said 'You know, you don't have to marry me if you don't want to now'

'Don't be daft Ray, you asked me before I was rich' she spoke quietly in a warm sincere tone and then pressed the CD button remembering that it was turned off as Roy Orbison started to sing 'Pretty Woman' and guess what? It resumed there again and they both laughed and started singing into one another's eyes; Julie suggested getting into the back seat for a quick wrestle but that idea quickly faded as some shoppers returned to the car next to them and began packing their days' shopping into the boot. So, on they drove into the darkness that like Julie's new found fortune seemed to appear suddenly and unexpectedly. It was on the Dundalk road that they slowed down because of the road works and were diverted towards the Newry Road, there was a big build-up of traffic as luck had it, otherwise they may not have spotted Glory B on the pavement surrounded by police.

'My God, is that Glory B....... and that looks like Ma Jess talking to the cops, oh jeeps there's been an accident...........

stop, stop, pull over' Julie's voice trembled, barely able to get the words out coherently but Ray understood and pulled over now blocking the traffic behind them; horns hooted and bumped in anger while Julie checked out if anyone had been injured and Ray checked out the damage to the car. His diagnosis was that the car could not make it to Dublin airport and the police confirmed this and advised Ray to move his own car before there was another accident.

Julie was keeping all her news until Gloria was safely in the car and they were on the main road once more heading for Belfast. Everyone rushed Gloria wanting to know how the Boston trip had ended and what was it that Charlie said to Glory B about some really good new that Gloria would have to break herself. This was all new to Julie, 'you...........were arrested oh my God..............right Ray..........we're going no further stop at the nearest hotel and I'm booking you all in for the night until I find out what's been happening' 'Uh.........' they all said in unison, 'you book us in and who's going to pay.......you'll never change Julie' laughed Gloria not really taking what Julie just said seriously but they all laughed when Roy pulled into the Fairview Hotel and parked the car in the 'residence only' section. Julie was the first out and she told the others in no uncertain terms 'right follow me or walk it home to Belfast by your selves'! The three girls followed like sheep; and always where there are sheep so also is there a shepherd and in that respect Mrs Jess laid the way or to put a different slant on the scene, the blind was leading the blind!

'Waiter' Julie clicked her fingers at a waiter now posturing an authoritative stance like a business woman in charge of organising a conference or something of that nature. 'A bottle of Champaign for the table and not your cheapest either and I want your best glasses to drink it from; oh yeah and one of those big ice buckets to keep it cool, you know the one's they have in the films'The waiter didn't seem to mind Julie's little show as he was used to this kind of behaviour from intoxicated older ladies; he had learned how to handle them without any nastiness and that always worked well for him. Gloria pulled Julie by the coat sleeve and whispered 'Please Julie, don't do this I've just been released from jail and now you're going to get us all arrested' Julie laughed and then as the Champaign cork was popped she stood on top of her chair and announced 'Friends I have an announcement to make.............' everyone in the bar stopped drinking and talking and look around to see who was making the speech. 'This has been the best week of my life' the chair was a little wonky and Ray moved quickly to steady Julie before she fell with the glass in her hand; she bent down and kissed him on the cheek before continuing. 'I just got the first real proposal from the best man I've ever met and I've accepted and if that wasn't good enough then, I find out I'm a widow' everyone laughed, ' And not only that but a millionaire widow as well.................drinks on the house' and glancing down at Gloria she mused 'I've always wanted to say that..............' Then jumping down off the chair aided by Ray, Julie lifted her glass and said 'To love true love'.

Gloria and Glory B both ran out of the bar and into the ladies for cover expecting to be arrested when the bill for the champagne arrived. Within seconds there was a crowd round Julie congratulating her as well as commiserating with her on her good fortune and off course the death of her husband.................

Again Mrs Jess came to the rescue. She made her way into the ladies and explained how this new drama had come about and how she and she alone had directed the new script from beginning till now and as her favourite detective would say 'I used my little grey cells to deduce what the real story line was and being from Belgium I took it from the beginning and followed it through to here and now, the end result is, my friend, once again (in a Belgium accent) parfacts-ion. I just love Hercule Poirot, that accent and his little curled up moustache, I could watch him every day, I just can't get enough of him, anyway, I did all my investigation on the internet again' Strange and stranger still was the fact that Mrs Jess was beginning to seem more like family now than just the woman from the Credit Union.

Returning from the ladies they were disappointed to learn that the restaurant was closed but the manager made sandwiches and brought them up to the rooms after everyone was checked in. Poor Ray had to spend the night alone as Julie and Gloria had so much to talk about; two weddings or one double? That now was the question but would Julie have the nerve to marry Ray and become a bigamist? A real bigamist! Both girls decided that there was only one possible line of action to take if Julie was to be married in St Peters and that was to get Mrs Jess on the case immediately. Even Julie acknowledged that Mrs Jess was becoming indispensable. She could find out if there were grounds for an annulment or some way of making her marriage to Ray legal. Mrs Jess and Glory B had already gone to bed before this part of the conversation came up; they were in the next room to Ray and could hear the television blurring though it didn't disturb either of them falling into a deep sleep as soon as their heads hit the pillows.

After exchanging all their good news stories to one another, both girls decided it was to be a double wedding in St Peter's Cathedral down Albert Street just off the Falls Road. The setting was magnificent; good enough for royalty and these two Falls Road girls were in their own community thought of as just that. It would be a lush extravaganza now that Julie was a millionaire and her gift to her lifelong friend Gloria was that she would pay for the whole wedding: dresses, cars, flowers, music the lot; everything except the one all-important thing that couldn't be bought and that was Julies' peace of mind; her first marriage, which it really wasn't (a marriage) as it was never consummated, was beginning to drag her down a little.

Amazingly, Mrs Jess came to the rescue again. She found out through the Births Death and Marriages in Summerset House that there was no such marriage registered to a Julie and Eric Trotter on neither the date nor place Julie had given her; to make sure she did a complete search of that whole decade for a record of a marriage certificate made out to them. But none existed. Mrs Jess concluded that a legal marriage didn't take place because the Justice of the Peace who supposedly married them, was a fake and Julie agreed that that was a real probability because Eric was so sly and in hindsight she believed he would have be capable of something like that. Great news for Julie, and also for Ray because he was that bit old fashioned even though he pretended not to be in case it would spoil his image of being a trendy free thinker!!!! Yes, you heard right, a trendy free thinker ummmmm.

Both couples agreed that they would like to be married before Christmas and so there was little time for the arrangements. The girls would fix the date and that was that. The Church date was no problem, but they realised that every hotel and club venue that catered for receptions was booked well in advance for the Christmas season so reluctantly they had to except the only date on offer otherwise the wedding would have to be postponed until January. Friday the 13th of December. Talking on the phone, Kelly and Glory B thought it was funny that their parents were sensitive about the number 13 though Kelly told Glory B that in America there was a condition called triskaidephobia and that it wasn't all that uncommon; that was why many hotels didn't have a room 13 or a 13th floor.

Mrs Jess said nothing about the date which was strange in itself, for she had plenty to say about everything else and now that she had theoretically adopted both Gloria and Julie and they had all become so close she thought it best not to point out that she was very superstitious and had a secret fear of the number 13; but she shared her hope with the girls that there would be snow in early December making everything perfect for a white wedding. Everyone was happy. There seemed no end to all this happiness that fate had bestowed so lavishly on both Gloria and Julie.

There wasn't much time to arrange things and Julie came up with a wonderful idea.

'Why don't I pay Mrs Jess to be our wedding planner? All brides are getting them these days. They take all the worry out of the organising a wedding and make it all run smooth. And besides it means we can spend more time getting beautiful; I've booked us in to Mount Eagles Hair and Beauty for our trial, and Maíre, the owner, said she'd come out on that morning and do our hair and make-up in the hotel, so I've booked the whole party with them. Henry and Ray can get a hair-cut up at the corner of Beechmount, I don't think they'll be bothered with spray tans or make-overs' the girls roared with laughter at the thought of someone spraying Roy, but, Roy could surprise them because he seemed to be game for anything; Henry was different, he was the strong silent type; sensual and sophisticated and not very demonstrative, at least he didn't used to be. Henry would be arriving the week before the wedding and would be staying at the Europa Hotel with his new bride, Mrs Gloria Dickson. Kerry would be staying with Glory B at the house.

Gloria and Julie were both delighted that now Mrs Jess was officially their surrogate mother; she had taken on the role instinctively and with grace. It was great to think that a mother figure would be with them throughout this whole new wonderful chapter in both their lives. Like Gloria, Julie's mother was also gone; not dead just gone, she had ran off with a delivery man from the Chinese take-away where she worked 10 years ago. Julie hadn't heard from her since, but it did feel good to have mother model there.

The day arrived when Henry and Kelly came to Belfast. Mrs Jess had arranged for a Falls Road black taxi to pick Gloria and Glory B up at their house and go up to the International Airport and collect them; what could go wrong with such a simple thing like hiring a taxi to get to the airport? Nothing, of course not, as long as you're not called Gloria! The taxi broke down at the entrance to the airport car park, causing a back log of traffic trying to get into the car park and also trying to get out which also cause a lot of road rage. Eventually, security had to be called and they got a pick-up truck to come and tow away the taxi from the vicinity least frustrated drivers who it seemed had turned into what only can be described as a potential 'lynch mob' got their way. The taxi man's name was Fred and he rang his mate Dave to come and pick them all up.

Henry and Kelly were relieved to be on the ground again because it was another tough flight with gale force turbulence for most of the 7 hour journey; the trauma of it disappeared at the sight of Gloria and Glory B. Both teenagers hugged and embraced like they were twins who had been separated at birth and now had found one another for the first time; as Gloria ran into Henrys open arms it seemed to both them to be happening in slow motion. Then in an instant, absolving heat ran through Gloria's entire body as Henry's strong arms wrapped around her like a soft blanket imbuing every sinew of her body. She had an overwhelming feeling of completeness.

Back in Belfast there was more good news from Henry but it would wait until they were unpacked and settled for the night.

Chapter 22:
The Day The Music Died

It was ironic. The two graves being in the same graveyard only a few feet apart. Ray's wife Maureen at the end of the row; Roslin and Moira two graves down in the same row. The sobs could be heard on the main road. The weather matched the mood. There was a very big crowd; everyone touched by a tragedy of such enormity.

Mrs Jess made a wonderful wedding planner. Everything going almost too smoothly. Henry announced the great news that Roslin and Moira had left him River Cottage and that was where he planned to spend the rest of his life if Gloria was happy enough to agree. She was overwhelmed and gladly agreed; it would be sad to leave Belfast immediately after the wedding; but the dawn of a new chapter in her life was about to begin and she looked forward to turning over each new page day by day, with Henry of course. Herself and Julie acknowledged to one another just how their lives had been changed in such a short time. 'Love changes everything' Julie said, 'in fact, I must tell Mrs Jess, to put that down for the first dance.'

'No way, I'm not dancing our first dance to that, it's too operatic, I was thinking more of Joe singing Unchained Melody, that's more us, don't you agree? Well we would never have met Henry or Ray if it hadn't been for Joe Dolan and country music, well sister, hurry up and agree' she joked knowing that the country flavour would win Julie over.

'Okay, you win, as long as Ray agrees, he'll not want to make an eejit of himself on the dance floor; he can dance to any Joe Dolan song, but also there is another reason why we have to choose our first dance song with care and that's because we don't know what song was played at Ray and Henry's first wedding, it would be awful if it were that, wouldn't it, in fact Gloria, we really don't know all that much about either of them, do we'?

'We know enough, enough to give them our heart, our deepest love without counting the cost if it doesn't work out the way we want it too, I love Henry and that's all there is to it.'

'You might love him, I mean I love Ray, but I still don't know what song he danced to on his wedding day.'

'Well, Henry wasn't into country music until he met me'

Julie cut in, 'Yeah, but what about his wife, what taste in music did she have, do you even know.............?.'

'Forget all that, I'm not interested, I only care about the here and now from now on, let's talk about our dresses'.

The dresses were almost ready; both girls bought them from Loretta's Bridal Shop just facing the end of Milltown Cemetery on the Falls Road. Loretta was a fantastic dress designer and maker; she was known for her creativity. She would take pictures of her clients and create a story around them which would inspire her to give each client an original one-off dress and head dress, unique to them alone. She was expensive, but worth every penny. Gloria could never have afforded the dress of her dreams if Julie wasn't paying for it. She was too proud to ask for Henry's help, money wise. The final fitting was three days before the 13th the day of the wedding. Everything was perfect, the dresses were covered in white dust type bags and brought down to the Europa and hung up inside the enormous wardrobe in Henry's room; room 14 as it happened. Henry promised that he would not under any circumstance have a peek; he was a man of his word so Gloria need not have explained that it would bring bad luck on them if he did peek.

Meanwhile Mrs Jess was busy organising the stag night and the hen night, she was old fashioned enough to still think it should all be innocent fun like tying people to lamp posts and pouring flour and eggs over them. There would be no strip a grams or dwarfs to surprise anyone or too much drink to take the good looks away from any of the wedding party; she told the girls it was the most important day of their lives and preparation was of the utmost importance. 'Every bride wants to look her best so go easy with the booze and have an early night. Rico and Peter will be driving Ray and Henry back to Donegal so Ray's car will be left in the hotel car park, and I'm picking up the suits at 4.55pm and will leave them off here so it's only a matter of putting them in Rico's car before they leave the next morning'. Looking into Gloria's blue eye she remarked that it was good that Henry and Ray had become friends and were spending their last night of freedom together; she emphasized that it was saving a lot of money just having the one limousine for the grooms, and it means that both would arrive at St Peter's at the same time. 'Amazing how everything has just fallen into place' she spoke to the girls like some sort of a professional fixer. 'St Peters will be packed, and Henry's friends in Boston will be able to watch him get married on the web-cam, oh this is all so exciting'. Mrs Jess just couldn't hide her elation at being such an important part of all this drama. She was the main organiser in fact and she wasn't going to let anyone who didn't already know this remain ignorant of that piece of information.

Tonight they were all gathered in St Peter's for the

rehearsal and confession. The bouquets were being made up of red roses and the Cathedral would also be decorated with red roses plus red and white ribbons tied around the end of each row of seats as far down as the 13th row on either side of the aisle. The Cathedral was such a magnificent place it needed no decoration to enhance its outstanding architectural splendour and no amount of cosmetics could compliment the already perfect colours and patterns of the tiled floor and columns. The altar was wide and would accommodate nicely the two wedding parties for the album photos.

Mrs Jess had brought her own camera and took some amazing photos on the altar. She instructed everyone how to stand and where to stand and she even got the two couples to hold hands and kiss as though they had just taken their vows for real. There was more laughing done in that half hour than in all the weeks that preceded the announcement of the weddings; and she also had Sean Green who would be singing during the wedding there as well. Sean was known all over Belfast as one of Clonard's best choristers. He was famous for singing every Christmas in Clonard Monastery, 'O Holy Night' and he sang it at the rehearsal; with unexpected tears in all their eyes he got a premature standing ovation. Julie said almost prophetically 'If Fr Hanna was here now we could just get married tonight instead of waiting,' and everyone laughed.

The following day was the busiest of all. Making sure everything that needed to be done was done. She had her check list out and was marking off from early morning. The only thing that Mrs Jess had no control over was the weather but what she did have was a direct line of communication with U.T.V. via email and was on to Valerie the weather girl every other half hour; in the end Valerie just posted Mrs J the updates as they come in to her department, it seemed the wiser thing to do.

Finally, before picking up the groom and best man's outfits Mrs Jess checked in with Conway Mill where the reception was to be held. The Mill didn't usually do wedding receptions though they had been thinking recently about spreading their services into that direction for the community for basically the Conway Mill was a community educational centre which had benefited many Belfast people of all age ranges including both Gloria and Julie. Everything seemed fine there and they all knew Mrs Jess from the Credit Union and were on first name terms. She spoke to Paddy the caretaker and Mary the Mill manager. They told Jean (Mrs Jess) to worry about nothing as everything was taken care of. The table settings were as she had requested and the caterers would be in from 4pm tomorrow evening to prepare the meals. Had the group of musicians from Donegal been in touch she asked Mary, 'Jean, they rang earlier and I gave them all the information they needed, plugs and lighting just general stuff, so please don't worry Jean, everything will be fine'. So with a skip and a hop in her step off Jean Jess went down town to collect the suits. She promised herself a soak in her new bath tub as soon as she deposited the suits safely at Gloria's.

Ten o'clock that night Mrs Jess was safely snoring in bed and the boys were getting drunker and drunker so drunk in fact that none of them would be able to drive all the way to Donegal the next day as arranged; it would be 5am before any of the boys even thought of going to bed.................... The girls had a great girlie night. Nails polished, back and feet massaged, skin tonics and a selection of false eye lashes to choose from for the morning of the wedding; perfection everything was perfection Gloria kept thinking and smiling and laughing because at last she was happy and she believed that Julie felt the same. And she did.

Rico and Peter could not be wakened they were in a dead sleep and Henry tried everything to get them up onto their feet, but nothing worked. The problem was that Ray had to be back in Donegal by 2.30pm to tie some loose ends up. He'd to see the limousine fellow and pay him and make sure that everything would be all right at the garage; he had employed his nephew to work the two weeks that he'd be away on honeymoon. And off course he wanted an early night (maybe) because he and Henry would be leaving Donegal at 9am sharp to arrive at St Peters for 11.30pm half an hour before the wedding. There would be no chance of Francie, the limousine man, hurrying if they were running late. Ray knew him well from card schools when they were younger and his greatest love was his Limos; he had two of them one grey and one black which the locals used to hire out for funerals. They had too much luggage to take with them so a bus was out of the question; the only alternative was to get a taxi back which would cost around £2oo. As fate had played such a large part in this whole story it now returned to play its final role.

Mrs Jess rang Henry to make sure that everything was on schedule. She was distraught at the idea of the grooms having to get a taxi all the way back to Donegal, after all, she was the main organiser and would have none of it. She proposed to meet them in Gloria's in one hour's time and chauffer them back safely to Donegal herself; she would have a quick doze when they arrived and return to Belfast before 8pm. That was the plan for there was no way she would contemplate letting any of them drive back in their still drunken state all the way to Donegal. It would be hours before Rico and Peter would sober up, so they could either get the bus home to Ballyshannon or stay in Belfast and leave for St Peters from Gloria's house. Gloria, Julie, Glory B and Kelly were all staying in the Europa and leaving from there in a white limousine. Things were back on track as they all said their good byes. Kelly embraced her father and told him that she was so happy that he was happy again and that she loved him. Henry felt like crying but he didn't. He was truly a very happy father, at last. As they were about to drive off Henry promised to ring Gloria before midnight and told her not to ring after that as though he wasn't really superstitious he didn't want to take any chances, so the next time he would hear her voice would be when she'd say 'I Do' again!

'I love you Henry Dickson' she blew him a kiss and turned away truly happy.

'What about me Mr Mechanic, don't I even get a squeeze'?

'Here babe', handing Julie a page from a jotter with writing on it. 'This is better than any squeeze you've ever had, I wrote it for you, it's a love song and I intend singing it to you tomorrow nighttttttttttttttttt, bye sweetheart, see you at the altar' and he blew her a kiss and she pretended to catch it in her hands.

'I'll report into the Europa as soon as I get back and let you know that they're both tucked up in bed for the night, bye' said Mrs Jess hurriedly and they drove off into the descending darkness of a cloudy sky.

The girls packed everything they would need and double checked twice. Mrs Jess had rubbed off on them for now they had a check list, so unbecoming of Gloria and Julie for they were not used to being so well organised. Glory B out of the blue asked if anyone had noticed if Mrs Jess was wearing her glasses; no one could remember but the thought niggled at the back of her mind for the rest of the day. The boys agreed that they were both still drunk and just wouldn't be able to get home by any means, they still needed to sleep. After a few hours they left the Europa and got a taxi back to Gloria's where they rung for a pizza and two cans of diet coke. They both fell asleep down in the living room for they just weren't used to the amount of drink they had consumed and couldn't cope with it.

It was before the two boys had arrived that Gloria found both mobiles in her kitchen still plugged in and charging. In their hurry Henry and Ray had forgotten them. Gloria hoped they would have the good sense to ring later from a land line. Two taxis arrived to bring the girls and all their cloths to the Europa; now it really was the night before their big day.

The girls were enjoying both chaos and tranquillity at the same time, it was a strange juxtaposition and how could either know that they would be in another juxtaposition before the New Year would start. Where were Henry and Ray and Mrs Jess, she'd promised to call or ring or contact them somehow when she got back. Was something wrong? At different times that's what each of them had been thinking. Glory B didn't want to frighten anyone by saying again whether Mrs Jess was wearing glasses or not. It was a stupid thought, she told herself over and over again. It was around 3am when the lights in room number 14 were turned out. Everyone happy and excited. Nothing could possible go wrong now, Gloria thought to herself as she prayed to St Jude her favourite saint; the saint of hopeless cases. What could go wrong, Henry loves me and I love him. 'Night everyone' she said in a whisper as she bent over to the other pillow where her daughter slept so peacefully and kissed her on the side of the head and thought, I hope someday you'll be as happy as I am now, baby.

In the other bed clutched tightly in her hand was the song Ray had written for Julie. She read it and reread it all night and tried to put a tune to it, but couldn't. No one had ever written anything for Julie before, and she felt so good that she was this important to someone now; to Ray. What a wonderful life we're going to have together after tomorrow, she kept thinking over and over. On the other pillow sleeping soundly and contented was Kelly. Kelly knew how much she was loved and knew the measure of her father's love was strong enough for both her and Gloria. Kelly was so happy with her father's choice this time of a wife and soul mate. Gloria was just perfect for her dad, she brought out the best of everything in him making him feel and behave young again; it was good that she felt comfortable with Gloria as a mother figure and of course there was a sister thrown in for good measure. All the ingredients for a happy future were there at this time and space in her life. They were truly blessed. This new way of life for Kelly here in Ireland was going to be a great adventure. Her dad had shared with her his hopes of setting up a small publishing business from River Cottage; she would help him all she could to make this new dream come true for him; for them.

Six a.m. and the rain was pelting heavily on the windows of room 14. The girls all woke up happy, though a bit disappointed by the weather. They expected Mrs Jess to appear any moment with their breakfast; instead they were greeted by two house maids who brought four red roses and presented one to each girl with their breakfast tray. Suddenly everyone came alive. There was a buzz in the room. This was going to be one of the happiest days of all their lives. Wasn't it?

Six thirty and the hairdresser and make-up technician arrived. Maíre and Aíne were sisters and loved their work; they could make anyone look beautiful and were known for their wedding creations. It was a creative service that they provided and they both loved what they did. The satisfaction of bringing out the best in a bride on her wedding day was always a goal they achieved; the fear of a bride not being happy with the 'look' or 'transformation' was always before the girls, but no one was ever disappointed except one very contrary bridesmaid, who was put in her place by the bride herself after several different attempts to make her beautiful and they were always well tipped, except on one occasion, but meanness doesn't take a rest on the biggest day of everyone's life. Does it!

By 10 am they still hadn't heard from Mrs Jess and they didn't expect to hear from either Henry or Ray for two reasons: one, they said they wouldn't ring before the wedding and also because they'd left the mobiles and probably couldn't remember the phone numbers; but Gloria thought to herself that they could have contacted them last night here in the Europa as it would be easy to get the number. It made Gloria a little uneasy thinking about why Mr Jess hadn't called at this stage also. Anyway they had so much to do right now and that was what was important. Mrs Jess had probably over-slept, she would be exhausted, and Gloria told Julie. Julie didn't take that much notice she was too busy telling the hairdresser what way to put the shade in her hair.

At last the wedding party was ready. The girls looked absolutely gorgeous, Maíre and Aíne had done a good job with the hair and make-up; they even helped Loretta get the four girls dressed. They had to go really carefully getting the dresses on avoiding any contact with the fake tan. Maíre took some photos for Gloria, for the before and after album she was intending to include with the main album. The excitement was tangible.

The photographer had positioned his camera on the wide stairway and captured beautifully the elegance of the occasion; guests in the hotel stepped aside as both brides held hands dissenting the stairs. The bridesmaids helped each bride get through the revolving doors at the entrance of the Europa and ushered them with ease into the waiting limo; the hotel manager wished them well as he and 4 house maids stood with large umbrellas the length of the pathway to the waiting limousine just in case an unexpected drop of rain should fall on the magical creation of two fairy-tale like brides; it was exactly 13 minutes to noon and the foul weather had subsided now for over an hour and everyone was grateful congratulating Gloria on her answered prayers. Once inside the limo she told them all that St Jude had never let her down yet. So now he would have an even bigger fan base.

As they drove slowly down Albert Street and turned into the St Peter's they saw Fr Hanna standing in the doorway very worried looking. They all noticed that Mrs Jess was nowhere in sight. Gloria knew instinctively that something was not right.

Fr Hanna approached the limo and told the girls not to get out just yet and not to worry either but the boys hadn't yet arrived. He said there was a traffic hold-up on the Glen Shane Pass due to the heavy snow there and that he had tried to contact Frankie the limousine man whom he knew well but was unable to get through to him. Perhaps they'd broken down somewhere. Perhaps.

The guests were all becoming anxious inside the Cathedral and began walking in and out and lighting up their cigarettes. No one knew what was going on and they really were beginning to get a more than just concerned. The girls bravely decided to go inside the Cathedral and tell the guests themselves what was happening. But before they disembarked from the limousine a police land rover turned into the square. A uniformed police man indicated over to Fr Hanna that he needed to speak to him, in private. The Limousine driver turned the engine off as Fr Hanna and the police officer approached the limousine. Fr Hanna opened the door on the left hand side and before he could even speak there was such screeching from the four occupants that the Cathedral emptied and people living across the tiny street and who had been watching the drama unfold came running like a herd of elephants and surrounded the limo. The police instantly formed a guard around it and tried to get people to withdraw back into the Cathedral.

There was nowhere to go. Nowhere to run or take shelter. The music died in each of them and now they were left with a harrowing silence.

As Mrs Jess raced up the M2 trying to reach Donegal in good time so she could have a rest before travelling back alone to Belfast in time to visit the girls and let them know everything was all right, except the weather of course, she felt one of her eye contacts move slightly. She still hadn't got the hang of putting the lenses in properly. Going along the Glen Shane Pass she sneezed and the contact disappeared somewhere to the side of her eye. Henry was sleeping in the back seat and Ray in the passenger seat. He was going over the song that he'd written for Julie; he wanted it to be so special for her on their wedding night. An oncoming lorry with full headlights on flashed at Mrs Jess indicating for her to turn her lights on as it was snowing and hard to see the oncoming traffic in the distance. The car was slightly blown across the narrow neck of the road and Mrs Jess lost control. The car tumbled down to the bottom of a ravine killing them all instantly. It would be 6am the following morning before the bodies were found and several hours later until their identity was established.

Friday 20th December. Donegal, Boston and Belfast came together via the web cam in St Peter's Cathedral. There really was wailing in the Chapel, it seemed to be contagious, people who didn't know Henry and Ray had become so caught up with these grief-stricken local girls that they took time off work and schedules to be with Gloria and Julie till the end; till the final flower was thrown on top of the coffins. Mrs Jess's funeral had taken place on Wednesday from St Paul's parish and there was not enough room for all the mourners, Cavendish Street was packed with the overspill of people from the Chapel and not a car could drive down through the crowd for over an hour. Gloria, Glory B, Julie and Kerry all held hands and sat in the front row of the Chapel alongside Mrs Jess's immediate family nursing their grief in silence. They were unable to follow the cortege outside to see it move slowly along the Falls Road on its way to Milltown Cemetery to its final resting place; it was in the older part of the grave yard over beside where the old Felons Club had stood many years before.

Kelly had agreed that Henry should be buried in with the O'Neill's; after all he was one of them. She had made no decision about what her immediate future would be. To return to Boston or stay on in Donegal, she just couldn't think that far ahead. But, after the 20th, decisions would have to be made. The only comfort was that now she wasn't alone. She had Gloria and Glory B. They would need each other. Julie felt totally alone, she felt that she had been stripped of everything and nothing more would ever matter. Nothing! How could it. Once you have true love in your life, noting else compares to it, nothing.

After the requiem mass they sat just staring out at the snow and wind through the steamed up windows of the back of the black limousine driven slowly by Frankie's brother Joe. Both coffins were carried in the limousine in front driven by Frankie; it stopped for 5 minutes at the spot of the accident and everyone got out and taking in the scene until it became too painful; moving off again they all had the same thought: the limousine that should have taken both men to their wedding was now taking them to their grave.

There were no formalities after the burials. The girls headed straight for River Cottage where a fire had been burning for days in preparation for their coming. They needed the stillness, the solitude and even the enduring loneliness that came with the shock of this sudden grief.

Now that both Gloria and Julie had money there was no need to rush back to Belfast. But, six weeks later they decided they had to return to sort their affairs out and do what they had to do. So off they went back to Belfast by bus. It took a week or so before Gloria felt she wanted to return to River Cottage to be with Kelly and Glory B, though Glory B would have to start studying again and

Kelly would have some decisions to make also. Henry's affairs in Boston were in need of sorting, his lawyer had been on to Gloria, she was his wife and so everything he owned now belonged to her and Kelly. They would need to go back to Boston to sort all those legal matters out. Gloria wondered if she would get past the immigration this time. But now her name was different, they mightn't notice???

Back in Belfast Julie thought seriously about her future for once. She had this money and knew she'd have to do something with it otherwise she could end up blowing the lot on men and booze. She hadn't changed that much since losing Ray, but she did consciously want to change her life style and she knew that she would never find anyone who would love her the way Ray had loved her. Maybe she should go over to Nashville and get someone to record the song that Ray had written for her; he'd called it 'A Song For Miss Julie'. Then out of nowhere came the idea that maybe she should try and trace Yuri's family in Russia and find out where he was buried and bring some flowers to place on his grave. She hadn't even bothered before to think about Yuri or what happened to his body after he died, he could still be in the morgue in Vegas for all she knew; it would be the right thing to do to find out what did happen to his body. Yes, that's what she would do now, this week in fact before the notion wore off. She discovered that his body had not been claimed and so she would do the right thing and go over claim it and bury it. Yes, she would give Yuri a proper burial. It was the least she could do for him.

Chapter 23: Life Must Go On

Gloria and Kelly made their plans to fly to Boston next week, Kelly was dreading the journey and what going back home to the empty house would entail. The house would have to be sorted, cloths burned or given to a charity. All Henry's private things gone through. It would be hard. At least she had Gloria to support her and they both loved Henry so much and through loving him had become close and now loved one another in a special and trusting way. Kelly agreed with Gloria that Julie should travel with them to Boston, stay a few days and fly out to Vegas and get Yuri's burial sorted, fly back and then book on the same flight return flight 'home'.

The three girls booked to fly out on the Wednesday before Valentine's Day. Gloria hadn't been feeling too well and went to see Doctor Smyth, the older of the two doctor Smyths, the younger was his son. By a great coincidence Julie had also an appointment with Doctor Smyth, the younger; for she also had been feeling a bit wheezy lately. Both girls staggered out of the surgery at almost the same time and both looked at one another in total disbelief, shock and elation at what their identical diagnosis was…………

As they sat side by side on the flight to America the Wednesday before Valentine's day the constant turbulence didn't bother them in the least because they were preoccupied with their own thoughts: Kelly with sorting the house, the finances and everything else that Henry took care of, herself included; Gloria and Julie both pondering on their good news that the Smyth doctors had given them; they each couldn't resist patting their stomachs as though they were eight months pregnant instead of 8 weeks. All three were anxious about the immediate future but two of them were experiencing that ultimate contentment of knowing that within their bodies lay their labours of love and that surely made all the difference to what the last two months had put them through.

There was a four hour delay when they landed at JFK terminal for their flight to Boston. They drank coffee and ate cake and biscuits for they weren't really hungry, just tired so they sat about reading magazines and Kelly got the Boston Globe, Henry's daily must read. Gloria was half asleep as they stepped into the plane minutes before take-off; the girls had all fallen asleep and were called twice over the intercom for boarding; the shock of waking to Fr Hanna's gentle shaking of Gloria's shoulders was like an extended nightmare when she opened her eyes and saw his face. He had spotted the girls earlier but didn't want to intrude in case he brought back all their sadness but when he heard their names being called for a second time he felt now was the time to approach them gently. There was no time for pleasantries or to ask where he spring from but they thanked him and were quickly ushered to the gate and had to run as if they were trying to catch a last bus; the passengers at the front of the plane stared as the girls were shown to their seats.

The pilot announced that they would be landing in approximately twenty minutes and that Boston had just experienced one of its worst blizzards in years. The girls didn't react to this information except to look at one another as if to say 'who cares' a blizzard was the least of their concerns. They were met at the terminal by Harry Eliot, an old friend of Henry's and it took them three hours before they reached the house where Harry's wife had the heating turned high and a meal on the table for the hungry travellers. It was Saturday before the girls began their dreaded tasks, but things had to be done and so they each began in their own way to deal with the jobs set out before them.

Julie flew alone to Vegas. She took pictures ever where alone the route from the airport so she would remember each pebble and tree and glitter that lined the streets, this time round. At the morgue she didn't look at Yuri's corpse but she did arrange for him to be brought to a little chapel and had a mass said there for him. The chapel was empty, Julie and the priest brought some life amid the marble statues and 18 pews. It did strike her how sad this was, not even a passer-by chanced to walk in; no one but Fr Smyth, Julie and her thoughts; not even an altar boy was there to help. The priest choose the readings: Ecclesiastes 1:1-8, then the Lord is my shepherd and the gospel was so short that Julie had just stood up and sat back down. There was no elegy at the end because there was nothing to say about someone she didn't know; yet how strange it was that she'd travelled all this distance to bury this person whose name she couldn't even pronounce and who had changed her life forever. She had forgotten about flowers, snowdrops she thought, if she had remembered. Then as she sat not listening to the priest but listening to an inner voice in her mind, she made a promise to Yuri, she promised him there and then that if her baby was a boy she'd call him Yuri, so Yuri, this unknown person, would be her baby's name sake. Like the feast day of a saint, she would always remember who her baby was named after and would never forget Yuri even though she could remember absolutely nothing about him. God rest him, she added. The body was cremated and Julie waited a few days on the ashes. She was going to trace his family and bring or send some of the ashes to them if they wanted them. Now back to Boston.

When Julie returned with the ashes the girls all cried. They cried not because of Yuri or his ashes but because they all needed to cry. Their grief exploded in the kitchen as they sat to have their evening meal. They each went their separate ways after a massive hugging session. Kelly and Julie to their rooms; Kelly played music and Julie rang Mrs Kelly in Fundoran to tell her the good news about the babies; really, it was just to hear her voice, any familiar voice would have done. Gloria was in the back garden in the little open sun house that Henry had made for Teresa long before she got sick; Gloria knew that there must have been so many happy hours spent there between Henry and Teresa, happy hours that she would never know with him but would always long for. There was a cane rocking chair covered in snow and a long stool protected with thick sheets of plastic wrapped around the legs and tied with cord. As Gloria removed the cord she could almost picture Henry tying it neatly and carefully so it could be undone with one slight tug; her life had been undone, untied with one huge tug and now what must she do, she thought, to put it back together and to go on?   Her heart began to race as she felt a slight flutter in her stomach; surely, she thought, it was too soon to feel movement like a little butterfly softly gliding through thin air; she sat on the stool and closed her eyes and imagined that she could hear music…Joe Dolan music and Joe singing Unchained Melody………..and then the most wonderful thing happened.

A hand touched her hand and he who the hand belonged, without effort, placed her hand on his shoulder, she felt a warmth run through her body from her toes upward; as she stood up she was gently pulled by two loving arms into a strong powerful body whose scent she recognised instantly and surrendering to the power of this intimate embrace she was led into a slow mystical-like dance that belonged to another time and place but now the time and place was here, in Boston. She didn't open her eyes for fear it would stop and disappear; she wished it would last forever; for some unknown reason she felt she was back reliving the time on the rocks in Donegal as she and Henry swam naked together between the rocks only now it was the moment and the music that plunged her through this time warp. She felt happiness again; knowing that when she would open her eyes that it would disappear……and it did. The music was interrupted by Julie voice. Julie related all Mrs Kelly's best wishes and this year's programme of events for the festival. But, from this moment on Gloria realised that she still had her memories and with them every emotion that she experienced with Henry.

Selling the house was beginning to take longer than first anticipate so Gloria and Julie returned to Belfast in good time for their first big scan in the Royal Hospital; neither wanted to miss their appointment to get the reassurance they needed that all was well with their babies. Kelly with the help of the Eliot's and as a short term solution decided to rent the house instead and also it made sense in case she couldn't settle in Ireland so she would still have a home in Boston to return to.

It had been a bad winter in Belfast. The snow lay for over a fortnight and there was a coldness that caused many people to have colds that seemed to go on and on, that's how it was for Julie and Gloria for most of the following 6 months; but everything must come to an end including pregnancy. From the security of the womb the baby eventually pushes forward into the wonder of the world. The most courageous step most of us will ever take.

Chapter 24: A New Beginning

Bags were packed from June, containing everything except the kitchen sink, as they say in Belfast. Neither girl wanted to be told what sex their baby was, Julie kept telling people who kept asking the question 'do you know yet what you're going to have?' 'Yes' I do know, it's going to be either a boy or a girl'. However, at the beginning of August the excitement really escalated in the Dickson/Jenkins house hold. Glory B had come back to help Gloria with the preparations for the birth of her new baby sister or brother; she didn't care which as long as it was healthy; it all sounded so wonderful that at last Glory B would have, really have, a family which would include Kelly as well. At the last weigh-in Gloria had put on two and a half stone, so for the first time in her life she was heavy and finding it hard to cope getting around. Her feet were very swollen and she was glad that Glory B was helping her with the shopping, even though she could now drive and had a blue Audi (which was great for all the toing and froing from Donegal) she still needed help.

Both babies were born 6 days apart. Julie gave birth first.

She had a healthy ginger baby boy weighing 7lbs. 6ozs. and she named him Yuri whom no one, except the few close friends who knew her story, could understand why she would give it a name like that. Julie intended to keep her promise to Yuri and it was something that baby Yuri might never need to know about.

The last few days were the longest for Gloria, she thought the day would never arrive when she would hold Henry's baby in her arms. It was a hard birth but the gas and air did wonders; quite a few times the midwife had to tell Gloria to go easy on it because it was making her go high. Strange thoughts began to occupy Gloria's mind; instead of thinking of Henry she thought constantly of Mrs Jess and how she had missed her and wished that she was there to hold her hand and support her in the delivery suite. Suddenly, she thought she was hallucinating when the midwife told her to start pushing, 'push, push, push' it sounded like a demand and Gloria was doing her best but the tiredness was holding her back, she had no energy; then standing at the foot of the bed as large as life stood Mrs Jess standing smiling and telling her it would be okay in just three pushes. Mrs Jess said as clear as day 'push' and Gloria pushed, then again 'push' and she pushed with all her might, then in a excited whisper Mrs Jess said 'one more push sweetheart, and it's over' and Gloria took a deep breath and pushed with all her might and the midwife exclaimed 'it's a girl, a beautiful baby girl congratulations Gloria……..a beautiful baby girl'.

Gloria wasn't able to sit forward to watch the cord being cut, she lay back and asked with closed eyes if the baby was all right. 'We'll just get her weighted and cleaned a bit before we give her over to you, mum'. Then the wonderful first cries of a new born baby that every mother wait for echoed deep in Gloria's heart. That first cry that tells a mother that her baby is healthy. The baby was set across Gloria's chest and when she opened her eyes she thought she saw Henry standing there wearing a white gown surrounded by a brilliant light and stroking their baby daughter and smiling. I'm calling her Henrietta after you Henry……………….and then the midwife took Henrietta from Gloria and began the task of making sure all the after birth was counted for.

Home was now permanently in Donegal. Gloria lived with her broken heart but made a good life for herself, Glory B, Kelly and Henrietta; they did well with the printing business. She remained best friends with Julie and Yuri og, as he became known in the Country and Western music scene. He sang around the country mostly songs Ray had written which Julie found hidden in the garage; he played the guitar and piano from an early age and could write his own music.

The End

www.ingramcontent.com/pod-product-compliance
Lightning Source LLC
Chambersburg PA
CBHW071756190726
48292CB00003B/1003